"Maybe We Could Bury The Hatchet,"

he murmured, feeling his way for the first time in his life. The self-confidence he'd always had with women was lacking tonight. He felt something new with Kate, and everything in him was fighting it. She confused him, disturbed him. She had to be sophisticated, but why did she sound so damned honest? She'd sworn once that she'd never lied to him, and he'd had to fight not to believe her. He couldn't believe her, because if he did... He stared at her, feeling something tingle inside him as her face colored. He couldn't prevent a warm, quiet smile.

His smile could open doors. She stared at him with wonder. He'd never smiled at her like that before. She returned it, with interest. "Perhaps we could," she said, her voice husky.

Dear Reader,

Season's Greetings!

This holiday season is one we associate not only with the hope for peace on earth and goodwill to all, but with love and giving. Perhaps the greatest gift is the gift of love—and that's what romance is all about.

The six Silhouette Desires this month are a special present from each author, and are for you, with love from Silhouette. In every romance, the characters must not only discover their own capacity for love, but the ability to give it fully to another human being. Sometimes that involves taking great risks— but the rewards more than compensate!

I hope you enjoy Silhouette Desire's December lineup, and that you will join us this month and every month. Capture the magic of romance—the gift of love.

Best wishes from all of us at Silhouette Books.

DIANA PALMER
Betrayed by Love

Silhouette Desire

Published by Silhouette Books New York

America's Publisher of Contemporary Romance

SILHOUETTE BOOKS
300 East 42nd St., New York, N.Y. 10017

Copyright © 1987 by Diana Palmer

ISBN: 0-373-05391-6

First Silhouette Books printing December 1987

America's Publisher of Contemporary Romance

Printed in the U.S.A.

Books by Diana Palmer

Silhouette Desire

The Cowboy and the Lady #12
September Morning #26
Friends and Lovers #50
Fire and Ice #80
Snow Kisses #102
Diamond Girl #110
The Rawhide Man #157
Lady Love #175
Cattleman's Choice #193
The Tender Stranger #230
Love by Proxy #252
Eye of the Tiger #271
Loveplay #289
Rawhide and Lace #306
Rage of Passion #325
Fit for a King #349
Betrayed by Love #391

Silhouette Romance

Darling Enemy #254
Roomful of Roses #301
Heart of Ice #314
Passion Flower #328
Soldier of Fortune #340
After the Music #406
Champagne Girl #436
Unlikely Lover #472
Woman Hater #532

Silhouette Special Edition

Heather's Song #33
The Australian #239

DIANA PALMER

is a prolific romance writer who got her start as a newspaper reporter. Accustomed to the daily deadlines of a journalist, she has no problem with writer's block. In fact, she averages a book every two months. Mother of a young son, Diana met and married her husband within one week: "It was just like something from one of my books."

One

He looked just as Kate remembered him, standing on the outside of the small gathering in front of the church. Jacob Cade had never mixed well. He might have his share of adoring women, thanks to his sizable fortune, but he seemed to treat everyone with the same impartial contempt. He was quietly smoking a cigarette, his dark gaze glancing toward the road where his niece was due to arrive any minute. And despite his indifference to the crowd, he drew women's eyes. He was darkly tanned and rugged, his powerful legs outlined by the superb fit of his trousers, his broad shoulders straining against the fabric of his suit coat. The hand holding the cigarette was lean and dark, and there were no rings on it. Jacob wasn't a sentimental man. He was an old-fashioned reactionary in everything from dress to attitudes, and he made no apologies for it. He didn't have to. He had enough money to make up his own rules as he went along.

"Lord of all he surveys," Kate muttered, glaring.

"Isn't he entitled?" Tom, her brother, laughed softly. "He's got enough fluttering female hearts in his pocket. Including yours..."

"Hush!" she bit off, nibbling on her lower lip.

"He doesn't know," he mused, glancing down at her. They were both tall, dark-haired and green-eyed. Although Tom, at twenty-eight, was four years her senior, they might well have been twins for the resemblance of their facial features. The same even, etched features highlighted both high-cheekboned faces, the faint remnants of a Sioux great-grandfather.

"I hate him," Kate said firmly, pushing a strand of hair back into the elegant French knot she'd twisted her long, straight hair into that morning.

"Sure you do."

"I do," she insisted. And at that moment, she really did. Jacob's sudden, violent dislike for her, which stemmed from an incident when Kate was eighteen, had put a severe strain on her friendship with Margo. It was odd, too, because Jacob had been good to the family when Kate was younger.

Kate and Tom had been adopted by their paternal grandmother after the death of their father. God alone knew where their mother was. She'd deserted them years before, and Kate had never stopped blaming her. The children had been badly scarred by the way their father had brought them up. Not even Grandmother Walker had known what they'd been through, because she hadn't been the kind of person who invited confidences. But she'd taken them into her home in Blairsville, South Dakota, just minutes from Pierre, the capital. Margo Cade had lived with her uncle Jacob Cade and his father, Hank, on Warlance since the unexpected death of her parents years before. When Kate and Tom Walker had come to Blairsville to live with their Grandmother Walker, the girls had become friends. They'd spent time at each other's houses since early high school. Now Margo was marrying, and although Kate had declined the honor of being a participant in the wedding, she couldn't get out of attending. Not even to spite Jacob Cade.

As if he sensed her presence, his lofty head turned, shaded by a very expensive cream-colored Stetson. He was immaculate in a deep gray vested suit, elegance personified in spite of the fact that Kate had seen him work cattle and knew the strength in that long, lean body.

His square jaw lifted and he smiled in her direction, but it wasn't a kind expression of greeting. He was declaring war without saying a single word.

Kate felt her neck tingle and she clutched the small white and jade bag that matched her pale green suit. She lifted her own chin, daring him. She'd spent her adult life doing that. It was like a defense mechanism, a programmed response that kept her from throwing herself at him. If she fought him, he couldn't get close enough to do her very vulnerable heart much damage.

She seemed to have loved him forever, all her life. Her dreams were full of him, her mind haunted with memories. Jacob, smiling at her from horseback as she learned to ride with Margo as tutor. Jacob, sitting quietly in the porch swing while she and Margo danced with their young suitors at summer parties on the ranch. Jacob. All her young dreams had been wrapped up in one strong, very virile man. And then, like summer lightning, Jacob had become her enemy.

Something had been growing between them from the time she turned eighteen. It had been in his eyes, a vague smoldering interest that frightened her even as it intrigued her. While she'd been growing up, he'd been an indulgent older-brother figure who'd included her in Margo's parties and outings as naturally as if she'd been part of the family. She'd never confided in him about her upbringing, of course. Kate had told no one, not even Margo, the truth about those anguished days. But Jacob had been kind to her. When Grandmother Walker had a stroke, it was Jacob who sat up all night with Kate in case she needed him. When Tom got in trouble at school for fighting, Jacob went to the principal and talked him out of expelling Kate's hotheaded brother. Jacob had always been there, like an anchor, holding everyone steady in the raging current of life. And Kate had grown to love him, attracted by his strength and kindness and the single-minded determination that seemed to cling to him like the spicy after-shave he wore. And then their relationship had all gone sour in the space of a single night, and her friend Jacob had suddenly become her worst enemy.

Kate and a boy she was dating had been invited to a pool party at Margo's house in July six years ago. After an hour of swimming, during which Kate had hardly been able to take her eyes off Jacob's incredibly sensuous body in white trunks, she'd gone to the bathhouse to change. Kate had just stripped off her bathing suit when she saw a rattlesnake coiled on the sunlit strip of concrete by the wall. With a phobia for snakes that dated from childhood, her mind had gone into turmoil. In her hysteria, she'd forgotten that she was undressed. She'd screamed and Gerald, her date, had come running. The snake had crawled away through a hole. She was shaking and sobbing and Gerald, helpless to do anything else, was just holding her. And Jacob had walked in and seen them like that—seen Kate's nude body being held close against Gerald's tall form that was clad only in brief trunks.

Maybe he'd have listened to her explanation another time, but Kate had grown angry at her reaction to Jacob's hard, fit body, as well as his blatant attention to Barbara Dugan, a beautiful and blond neighbor. And she'd gone to Gerald in the pool and had kissed him in a totally adult way, an action that Jacob had seen. He could hardly be blamed, Kate realized, for thinking so badly of her. She was shocked at her own behavior, but she was confused at the force of her attraction to Jacob and her inability to do anything about it.

She thought she'd never forget the way Jacob had looked at her, his black eyes filled with contempt, his face devoid of any expression while Gerald, unnerved by Jacob's unexpected fury, stumbled over an explanation that sounded too dispirited to be convincing.

Every word of it was true, but Jacob hadn't listened to them. It was almost as if he'd wanted to believe only the evidence of his own eyes. That had been the last time she'd been welcome at Warlance. Despite Margo's pleading and threats, Jacob had stood firm. He didn't want his niece associating with a woman like Kate, he'd said. He'd thrown Gerald off the property on the spot, sending him away without a word.

Before Kate had joined Gerald in the car, she and Jacob had a grandfather of a brawl, one so hot that even old Hank Cade hadn't mixed in it. He'd moved out of earshot, watching his son raise hell while Margo tried desperately to referee.

"You won't listen, will you?" Margo had said, defending Kate. "It was innocent! There was a snake in the bathhouse!"

"Sure," he replied, his voice colder than Kate had ever heard it, his hard glare silencing Margo immediately.

Kate had clenched her hands by her sides, blazing with bad temper and hurt pride. "Go ahead, then, believe I'm that kind of woman, even when you know I'm not!"

"I thought you were a little saint," he replied curtly, his gaze chilling her, "until tonight when your halo slipped and I saw you grow up."

She didn't understand the way he'd phrased it. Not that, or the unreasonable contempt in his tone. "Jacob, I'm not like that! And I don't lie—I've never lied to you!"

"I watched my mother go that route," he said in a haunted tone. "One man after another and denying the whole time that she'd ever cheated on my father. One day, she ran off with her latest lover and never came back. I've never forgotten what a hell she made of my father's life. I raised my niece to have a conscience and a sense of morality. I'm not having Margo exposed to women like you. Get off my place and keep off."

Margo had gritted her teeth, but her eyes had been eloquent as they apologized to Kate silently. Jacob in this mood was dangerous. And Kate understood.

"You won't listen," Kate said quietly. "I'm sorry, because I'd never willingly lie about anything. There's so much you don't know, Jacob," she'd added, her smile wistful and bitter. "Not that it would matter, I guess. You don't think people should stoop to being human. You want perfection in every way."

"Your grandmother would be ashamed of you," he said roughly. "She didn't raise you to be a loose woman. She never should have let you go to work for that damned newspaper."

Kate had gotten a summer job with the local weekly paper, and Jacob had been against it from the start, unlike Grandmother Walker, who thought women should do what they pleased in business.

Her job had been just something else he disapproved of. Lately she had seemed to get on his nerves, to antagonize him for no obvious reason. This was the last straw, though. Kate knew that he'd never forget or forgive what he thought she'd done in that bathhouse. He'd stripped her of her pride and self-confidence—and without even raising his voice. That was Jacob. Always controlled. He never really lost his temper; he used it.

"I like reporting," she replied. "In fact, I plan to make a career of it. And now I'll be pleased to decontaminate your ranch by leaving it. I'm only sorry the snake didn't bite me, because then at least you'd believe me. Goodbye, Margo. I'm sorry your uncle won't let us be friends anymore."

"You can make book on it," he replied, lighting a cigarette with steady fingers while his dark eyes glared at her.

He'd given Kate an appraisal that spoke volumes before he turned and walked away without a single word.

That had been six years ago. In the time that followed, Kate had gone to journalism school for a couple of years and wound up working for a Chicago daily newspaper. She hadn't known anyone in Chicago, but Tom had a friend there, and the friend had pulled a string or two. Kate liked the big city. It was the one place she might be able to forget Jacob.

Jacob had relented just a little afterward. Kate was still unwelcome at Warlance, of course, but he'd stopped short of forbidding Margo to talk or write to her. Once Margo had even invited her to the ranch for a weekend, apparently with Jacob's blessing, but Kate had refused. She was still hurt from Jacob's unreasonable treatment. She hadn't even wanted to come to the wedding. But since it was being held in Blairsville, not on the ranch, she felt fairly safe. And Tom was with her. Dear Tom. She hated her own cowardice, but she clung to him.

"You're a reporter," Tom was saying, breaking into her silent reveries. "You've won awards. You're almost twenty-five years old. Don't let him intimidate you. It will only make him worse. You can't buckle under with people like Jacob. You ought to know that by now."

"Knowing it and using it are two different things. And I do hate him," she muttered, glaring at Jacob as he turned to speak to a nearby couple. "He's so lordly. He knows everything."

"He doesn't know you're still a maiden, I'd bet," Tom chuckled, "or he'd never have accused you of messing around in the bathhouse with that poor nervous little boy."

Her face flamed. "I'll never forgive him for that."

"He doesn't know what kind of upbringing we had," Tom reminded her. "He never knew our folks, remember. We were living with Grandmother Walker by the time you met Margo and became friends with her."

She smiled softly. "Granny was a character. Even Jacob Cade didn't run over her. You remember, he tried to make her forbid me to go on that overnight camping trip with Margo just a few months before he told me to stay off the ranch forever. Granny informed him that I was eighteen and could go where I pleased." She frowned. "I never did understand why he was so against it. We had a great time. There were college boys along, too, and chaperons... It was very well behaved."

"It should have been, since he went along as a chaperon," Tom mused.

"That was the only bad thing about the whole experience," she muttered.

"Liar. I'll bet you spent hours sitting and watching him," he whispered.

Her eyes fell. Of course she had. One way or another, she'd spent her entire adult life mooning over the only man in the world who hated her. She wondered sometimes if she hadn't deliberately worked toward a career in reporting just as an excuse to leave Blairsville and get away from him. Chicago was as far away as she could manage. Now that Grandmother Walker was dead and Tom was working for an ad agency in New York, there was no reason to stay in South Dakota. But there was every reason to escape; she had to keep away from Jacob. Kate had never fancied growing old with her heart in shreds from his day-to-day indifference. Living in Blairsville, she'd have seen him frequently, and heard about him even more often. That would have been too painful to contemplate.

Her attention was caught by a flash of red as Margo's little sports car drew up at the curb, driven by her fiancé, David. He hopped out, resplendent in his white tuxedo with a red carnation in the lapel and a red cummerbund. He was fair, tall and very attractive.

"About time," Tom chided as the bridegroom paused beside them. "Where's Margo?"

"Arriving momentarily with her grandfather. I hope," David added with a tiny shudder. "Have you seen Hank drive?" he groaned.

"Yes," Tom replied with a sigh. "He's almost, but not quite, as bad as Jacob."

David laughed, and Kate hated herself for hanging so eagerly onto any tidbit of gossip about the man she loved.

"Jacob wrecked three cars before he got through college," Tom mused. "Our grandmother wouldn't let Kate go to Warlance unless Margo drove."

"I expected to see you both at the house," David began.

Kate was searching for an excuse when a shadow fell over her, and her heart ran wild. It was like radar; she always felt Jacob before she saw him.

"So there you are," Jacob said, joining the group. He didn't even look at Kate. "Hello, Tom. Good to see you." He extended his hand and shook the younger man's firmly. There was only about four years between the two men—Jacob was thirty-two—but Jacob seemed a generation older in his attitudes. "Where's Margo?" he asked.

"On the way, with your father at the wheel, I'm afraid." David sighed. "Well, it's not my fault," he added defensively when Jacob glared at him. "We couldn't fit that expensive wedding gown you bought her into the car without taking it off first." He grinned wickedly. "I was all for that, of course, but Margo seemed to feel that it would shock the congregation."

Jacob wasn't amused, but Tom had to bite his lip. So did Kate, despite the tense undercurrents.

"My father is half-blind with cataracts he won't have removed," Jacob said coldly. "He's got no business driving at all."

"Hurry, let's rush and phone the state police," David offered. "What a great opportunity to have his license pulled."

Tom couldn't help it. He laughed. "Sorry, but I have this mental picture of the entire wedding party bailing the old fellow out of jail—"

Kate clung closer to Tom's sleeve. "There they are," she murmured, nodding toward the road, where a big Lincoln with Hank behind the wheel was just nudging against the curb and stopping.

"See?" David laughed as Margo got out of the car, escorted by a tall, silver-haired man who was an older version of Jacob but without his fiery temper and cold, domineering manner. "No broken bones, no ripped fenders, everything intact. Hmm, she does look a bit pale."

"Probably the stark terror of realizing she's marrying a crazy person," Kate offered, grinning at David.

"I'm not crazy." David defended himself with mock solemnity. "Just because I once, only once, went with Margo to a male strip joint—"

"A what?" Jacob demanded fiercely.

David actually flushed. "Uh-oh." He moved away. "Excuse me, have to rush. Getting married today, you see." He vanished.

"A what!" Jacob glared at Tom.

"It's a place where men take off their clothing while women wolf whistle," Kate offered, adding fuel to the fire. "Very educational." Well, she'd heard that they were, anyway. Kate herself wouldn't be caught dead in such a place, but Jacob might as well think she would, if it needled him.

Jacob's dark eyes were frankly insulting. "I can't imagine that you'd need any educating."

"How sweet of you to say so," Kate said with a demure smile.

The taller man didn't bother to reply. "See you inside," he told Tom, and walked off.

"Whew," her brother sighed as they started toward the rest of the congregation who were entering the church. "Talk about heat!"

"He hates me," she sighed. It had been a good act, but only an act. Inside, she was bleeding to death and no one could even see.

"I wonder if Jacob really knows what he feels for you, Kate," Tom remarked quietly.

But she didn't answer him. She walked up the steps and into the church, thinking as she went how very fortunate Margo was.

Two

The wedding was so beautiful that Kate cried. Sitting quietly near the pulpit, listening to the words that would bind David and Margo together, she felt a sense of loss for herself. She'd never hear those words, never know the overwhelming joy of pledging her life to a man who would love her back with equal passion.

Involuntarily, her eyes turned toward Jacob where he towered over David at the altar. He took such occasions seriously, and this one must have touched him, because he and his father had been responsible for Margo since her tenth birthday. As if he sensed her watching him, he glanced over his shoulder, his dark eyes catching hers. She didn't wait to read the expression in them; she quickly dropped her gaze to her lap. Such encounters with Jacob always left her feeling inadequate.

At last it was over, and the wedding guests gathered outside to pelt the lucky couple with dainty little sachets of rice. Margo reappeared shortly in a neat white linen traveling suit. David was at her side, his tuxedo exchanged for a sports coat and casual shirt and slacks. The newlyweds looked young and wildly excited, hardly able to keep their eyes from each other.

"Be happy, darling," Kate murmured, hugging Margo warmly before she climbed into the red sports car beside her new husband.

"I will. I really will." Margo glanced over Kate's shoulder. "Uncle Jacob looks as if he'd like to bite somebody."

"Probably me." David chuckled as Margo got in beside him. "I told him about our jaunt to the male strip joint."

"How could you?" Margo wailed. "He'll kill us!"

"He'll have to catch us first." David put the small car in gear with a wicked grin. "Goodbye, Kate. Goodbye, new Uncle Jacob!"

And they were gone before Jacob could say a single word.

Kate couldn't resist baiting him. It was a way of life. She glanced up at his strong, hard face with a small laugh. "Were you going to have a brief word with Margo about what to expect on her wedding night, Uncle Jacob?" she murmured discreetly, although they were away from the other wedding guests.

He glared down at her. "You might have done that yourself. I doubt if my experience would match yours."

"You might be surprised," she said.

He bent his tall head to light a cigarette, but his dark eyes never left hers. "Margo invited you to come down for a few days before the wedding to visit with her. You refused. Why?"

"Because of you," she said without hesitation. "You threw me off Warlance over six years ago and told me to never come back."

His broad shoulders shrugged, and muscles rippled like rapids in a river. He was overpowering this close—vividly male, abrasively masculine.

He stared down the long, straight road. "A few days after that pool party, one of the gardeners killed a rattlesnake in the bathhouse," he remarked quietly.

"Nice of you to apologize when you found out," Kate replied, almost shaking with suppressed rage. He could have admitted that six years ago, but he'd kept it to himself.

He looked down at her, and his eyes were cold. "There was a snake. But you were still naked in that boy's arms."

"I was scared to death, too," she returned. "I hardly knew what I was doing." She dropped her eyes to his tie. It was nice. Navy blue with red diamonds. "Never mind, Jacob. Think what you like. You always do, regardless of the evidence."

"Why did you go to Chicago to work?" he asked abruptly, his dark eyes glittering down at her through a wisp of cigarette smoke. "Why not Pierre?"

The question shocked her. It wasn't like him to seek her out deliberately and start talking. He never had before, at least.

She stared up at him helplessly, every single thought gone out of her head except how handsome he was. Darkly tanned, even-featured, he would have caught more sophisticated eyes than Kate's. She swallowed.

"Chicago is big," she said inanely, still staring up at him with wide, soft green eyes.

"So it is," he agreed quietly. As they stood together without a word for long, static seconds, he searched her face, probing softly, and she felt her knees giving way.

"The ... wedding ... It was nice," she choked out finally. Her heart was trying to burst under the intensity of his long stare.

"Very nice," he agreed, his voice deeper than she remembered it.

"They're going to Jamaica," she added breathlessly.

"I know. Dad and I gave them the trip for a wedding present."

"They'll enjoy it, I'm sure." This was ridiculous, she told herself. She was a reporter, a whiz with words, even her city editor said so. Why was she stammering like a grammar school kid?

He was still looking in her eyes as if he couldn't get enough of just gazing at her. This is insane, she thought. Jacob was her worst enemy.

"You've changed," he said finally. "You're more mature. More poised. What do you do at that newspaper you work for?"

"Politics," she said without thinking.

"Do you like it?"

"It's very exciting," she confessed. "Especially the elections. You get involved, even though you try to report impartially. I think I jinx the candidates, though," she added with a sheepish smile. "Mine always seem to lose."

He didn't return the smile. He lifted his cigarette to his mouth again while Tom shifted restlessly in the background. It was unusual for Jacob and Kate to talk without looking for weapons.

Jacob dropped his cigarette and ground it out under his expensive boot. His dark eyes searched hers. "I suppose you and Tom will go back tonight?"

She nodded. "We have to. I've got an interview first thing in the morning."

His cleft chin lifted and he narrowed his eyes, searching hers. "That boy, Kate..."

"I never lied to you, Jacob," she whispered.

The change in his face was faintly alarming, explosive. The muscles in his jaw tautened, his eyes went black. "I can't remember a woman ever saying my name the way you do," he said half under his breath.

She had to fight from flinging herself into his arms and begging for his mouth. She looked at it now with aching hunger, followed its chiseled perfection with eyes gone misty from all the years of hopeless longing. Would it never end, this longing for him? He'd never touched her, never kissed her, in all the years she'd known him. She dreamed about it, about how it would feel. But it would never happen.

"I have to go," she said miserably.

His chest expanded slowly, as if he was taking a deliberate breath. "Yes," he said finally. "So do I. I've got to catch a train to New York for meetings about some cattle futures."

He was taking the train because he didn't trust airplanes, she recalled with a faint smile. He never flew unless it was a matter of life and death.

He did look every inch a businessman, all right. Her eyes adored him one last time. Now that Margo was married, she might never see him again. The thought was vaguely terrifying. That fright seeped into her expression, puzzling the tall man beside her.

"What is it?" he asked, his deep voice almost gentle.

"Nothing." She clutched her purse closer. "Well . . . I have to go."

"You said that."

She shrugged and smiled faintly. "Yes."

He didn't reply and she turned slowly toward Tom, her heart sinking.

"I get to Chicago from time to time," he said unexpectedly.

She turned, nervous and breathless. "Do you?"

His chin lifted again and his eyes lingered on her face speculatively. "I might take you out to dinner one night."

She tried not to let her enthusiasm show, but she failed miserably. "Oh, I'd like that," she whispered.

"So would I." He let his eyes run slowly down the length of her body, admiring it with sensuous candor. "You've been off-limits for a long time, Kate," he mused, catching her gaze suddenly. "But Margo's out of the picture now; there are no more barriers."

She didn't understand. "What?"

He laughed softly, but it wasn't humorous. "We'll talk about that sometime. Are you in the phone book?"

"Yes," she replied. "My first initial and my last name are listed. I'm in the Carrington Apartments."

"I'll find you." He turned away to glance at Tom, who was still hovering. "Can I give you a lift to the airport?"

Tom joined them, smiling. "Thanks, but we've got a rental car."

"Those do come in handy. I've got a train to catch. Nice to see you again, Tom." He extended his big, lean hand and shook Tom's. Then he glanced back at Kate with a peculiar smile. "I'll see you."

She nodded. "Have a nice trip."

"I usually do." He turned and strode off, lighting another cigarette on the way, while Kate watched him with her heart in her eyes.

"If he sees the way you're looking at him, the game's up," Tom teased, holding her by the arm to propel her to the Ford he'd rented. "Come down out of the clouds, girl. We've got to make tracks if we're going to catch our plane on time."

"Yes, of course."

"What were you talking about?" he probed.

"He comes to Chicago on business sometimes," she murmured, glancing out the window and catching sight of Jacob as he passed them in his big Lincoln. She sighed. "Oh, Tom. He wants to take me out to dinner."

"Horrors," Tom exclaimed, pulling out into the street. "Watch out."

She frowned. "Why?"

"For God's sake, Kate. Margo's married and you've just gone on the endangered-species list. Or hasn't it occurred to you that he's wanted you for years?"

Her heart skipped. "Me?"

"Of course, you," he grumbled. "Jacob looks at you as if you were a juicy steak with his name branded on it. He always has. My God, if it hadn't been for the fact that you and Margo were best friends, he'd have seduced you years ago."

"It isn't like that—"

"The devil it isn't," he persisted. "Listen, honey, I'm a man. I know how men think. Now that Margo's out of the picture, Jacob feels free to pursue you, and I do mean pursue. He's never believed you about that Gerald boy; he never will. As far as he's concerned, you're a city sophisticate, not a shy little country maiden. So watch it. I've heard stories about that man all my adult life, and I believe them. He's a mature, sophisticated man with a line of women an arm long, and he doesn't drag his feet. Did you really think that he was celibate all this time?'' he added as he caught a glimpse of her shocked face.

"Margo said he never brought anybody home." Her voice faltered.

"Of course not—he wouldn't flaunt his conquests around Margo! Or don't you remember what a peculiarly old-fashioned man he is when it comes to women and liberation?''

"I remember all too well," she sighed, leaning back against the seat as she recalled his reaction that long-ago afternoon to the sight of her in a man's arms.

"Then keep it all in mind. He isn't in the market for a wife, honey," Tom added softly. "I know how you feel about him. But don't let your emotions blind you to the truth. What he wants is to satisfy a temporary hunger. When he marries, if he marries, it will most likely be Barbara Dugan, whose father owns the Double D Ranch adjoining his. It will be a nice merger and double his holdings, and Barbara isn't half bad to look at.''

"Yes, I suppose you're right, Tom." She felt sick all over. How was she going to manage to say no to Jacob when the time came and he asked her out? She loved him so desperately that even a few minutes of his company would last her starving heart for years. She looked at her brother helplessly. "Maybe he cares about me, a little.''

"Maybe he does," he said. "But don't you ever forget his mother and how he feels about the whole female sex because of her. He'll never marry a woman he's slept with.''

She flushed despite herself and turned her eyes back to the road. "His mother ran around with everyone, from what Margo said. And poor old Hank just sat and did nothing."

"She was a wild woman, Grandmother said. Nothing like Hank, who was easygoing and pleasant and not very ambitious. She got tired of having nothing and went after the rainbow." He sat deeper in the seat as they approached the city. "I guess she found it eventually. She married that Texas oil magnate and lived happily until she died. But Jacob hated her for what she did to him and his father and brother, and he hated the humiliation of having to live down her reputation."

"He hasn't had a good impression of women," Kate said quietly.

"Keep that in mind. He won't let his emotions get in his way."

"I'll keep it in mind," she promised.

He started to say something else. But he just smiled and reached over to pat her hand where it lay on her purse. "How about some lunch before we catch the plane? What would you like?"

"Something adventurous," she said, quickly following his lead. "How about squid?"

"Yech! How about something civilized?"

She sighed. "Steak and potatoes, I guess?"

"Civilized," he emphasized. "Like a McDonald's hamburger!"

"Now, that's civilized." She laughed. "Drive on!"

Tom kept her mind occupied with wild tales about his advertising job in New York, and about some of his more eccentric clients—like the soap magnate who liked to listen to Tom's presentations while taking bubble baths with a background of Mozart pieces, or the chewing gum heiress who brought her purebred collies to each meeting, to make sure her beloved pets approved of the ad campaigns.

Her brother was the only living relative she had now, and she tended to lean on him the slightest bit. She felt guilty at her own rebellious feelings when he criticized Jacob. Perhaps it was a fair warning, although she didn't like facing that possibility. She preferred to think that Jacob had only just noticed her and wanted a new beginning for the two of them. So that was what she was going to think, whether or not her older brother approved.

She waved him off to New York soon after they landed in Chicago, and caught a cab back to her apartment. The sense of loneliness that washed over her was nothing new. She felt alone every time she walked away from Jacob. She wanted him, so badly. Would it be very wrong to have an affair?

Her father's harsh recriminations came back on cue. That kind of woman, he'd raged, his daughter wasn't going to become. He was going to make sure of it. And he'd harped on permissiveness, on the ills of modern society, on the terror of unwanted children, until he'd poisoned Kate's young mind. When she and Tom were in high school and went to live with Grandmother Walker, there was no free will left. Kate often wondered what her life would have been like if only her mother hadn't left. Her mother had been like Jacob's, according to her father. Her father had often sworn that Kate wasn't really his child, anyway, but she and Tom looked so much alike that Kate tried not to think too hard about it. That part of her life was over, anyway. Looking back would only bring more nightmares.

As she got into bed, drowsy with weariness, she wondered if Tom had been right, and Jacob really had wanted her for years. She flushed with the memory of that long, speaking look he'd drawn over her body. Yes, he did seem to want her now. And she wanted him, wanted the union, the total belonging of being in his arms with nothing between them.

She turned into her pillow, burning with new desires. If only Jacob had believed her about that misunder-standing... But on the other hand, mightn't knowing the truth turn him off completely? If Tom was right, and Jacob preferred sophisticated women, wouldn't he be likely to walk away from Kate if he knew she was a virgin?

On that troubling thought, she closed her eyes and slept.

Three

——

The brief vacation from work seemed vaguely unreal to Kate once she was back at her desk at the Chicago daily newspaper where she worked. And, as usual, everything was in a virtual frenzy of confusion.

Dan Harvey, the city editor, was the only man functioning at full capacity. There was an unwritten law somewhere that city editors didn't fall victim to insanity. Kate often wondered if that was because they caused it.

Harvey presided over the newsroom, and he managed story assignments as if it were delicate choreography. In the hierarchy of the newsroom, there was a state news editor who dealt with breaking stories outside the city and worked with the few stringers, or correspondents, the paper maintained outside the city proper. There was a feature editor, a wire services editor, a society editor, just to name a few, with all of them—Harvey included—under the watchful eye of the managing editor, Morgan

Winthrop. Winthrop was a veteran reporter himself, who'd worked his way up the ranks to his present position. Next to the editor in chief, James Harris, and the publisher, Winthrop was top man in the paper's power structure.

At the moment, Kate was under Harvey's gimlet eye while she finished the last, grueling paragraph in a rapidly unfolding political story about a local alderman who'd skyrocketed to fame by spending a week in a local neighborhood besieged by crime.

It was just hard to think with a tall, bald man standing over her, glancing pointedly at his watch and tapping his foot. She hoped he'd get bunions, but he probably caused those, too.

"Okay." She breathed a sigh of relief and showed him the screen on the terminal.

"Scroll it," he instructed, and began to read the monitor from his vantage point above her left shoulder as she started the scrolling command. Since the word processor screen would only show a portion of the whole story, this command was used to move each line up so that another appeared at the bottom until the end. Harvey pursed his lips, mumbled something, nodded, mumbled something else.

"Okay, do it," he said tersely and left her sitting there without a tiny word of praise.

"Thanks, Kate, you did a great job," she told herself as she entered the story into the memory of the computer. "You're a terrific reporter, we love you here, we'd never let you go even if it meant giving you a ten-thousand-dollar raise."

"Kate's getting a ten-thousand-dollar raise," Dorie Blake yelled across the bustling city room to Harvey. "Can I have one, too?"

"Society editors don't get raises," he returned with dry humor, and didn't even look over his shoulder. "You get paid off by attending weddings."

"What?" Dorie shot back.

"Wedding cake. Punch. Hors d'oeuvres. You get fed as a fringe benefit."

Dorie stuck out her tongue.

"Juvenile, juvenile," Harvey murmured, and went into his office and closed the door.

"Tell Mr. Winthrop that Harvey goosed you behind the Linotype machine," Bud Schuman suggested on his way to the water fountain, his head as bald as Harvey's, his posture slightly stooped, his glasses taped at one ear.

Dorie glared at him. "Bud, they took out the Linotype machine ten years ago. And our managing editor doesn't listen to sob stories. He's too busy trying to make sure the paper shows a profit."

"Did they take out the Linotype machine?" he asked vaguely. "No wonder I don't have anyplace to put my ashtray..."

"Honest to God, one day he'll lose his car just by not noticing where he parked it." The older woman shook her red head.

"He's still the best police reporter we have," Kate reminded her. "Twenty-five years at it. Why, he took me to lunch one day and told me about a white-slavery racket that the police broke up here. They were actually selling girls—"

"I should be lucky enough to be sold to Sylvester Stallone or Arnold Schwarzenegger," Dorie sighed, smiling dreamily.

"With your luck, they'd sell you to a restaurant, where you'd spend your twilight years washing plates that had

contained barbecued ribs," Bud murmured as he walked
back past them.

"Sadist!" Dorie wailed.

"I've got three committee meetings, and then I have a
news conference downtown." Kate shook her head,
searching for her camera. "Alderman James is at it
again." She grinned. "He's just finished his week in the
combat zone and is going to tell us all how to solve the
problem. With any luck, I'll get the story and have it
phoned in to rewrite in time to eat supper at a respect-
able hour."

"Do you think he's really got answers, or is he just
doing some politicking under the watchful eye of the
press?" Dorie asked.

Kate pursed her lips. "I think he cares. He dragged me
out of a meeting at city hall and enlisted me to help a
black family in that ward when their checks ran out. You
remember, I did a story on them—it was a simple computer error, but they were in desperate straits and sick..."

"I remember, all right." Dorie smiled at her. "You're
the only person I know who could walk down back al-
leys at night in that neighborhood without being bothered. The residents would kill anybody who touched
you."

"That's why I love reporting," Kate said quietly. "We
can do a lot of harm, or we can do a lot of good." She
winked. "I'd rather help feed the hungry than grand-
stand for a reputation. See you." She slung the shoulder
strap of the camera over her shoulder, hitched up her little laptop computer in its plastic carrying case, and
started off. She could use the computer for the committee meetings and even the alderman's breaking story. She
had a modem at home, so when she fed the notes into it,
she could just patch them into the newspaper from the

comfort of her living room. It certainly did beat having to find a phone and pant bare facts to someone on the rewrite desk.

Unfortunately for Kate, the little computer broke down at the last committee meeting, just before she was to cover the alderman's speech. She cursed modern science until she ran out of breath as she crawled through rush-hour traffic toward city hall. There was no time to go by the paper and get a spare computer; she'd just have to take notes by hand. Great, she muttered, remembering that she didn't have a spare scrap of paper in her purse or one stubby pencil!

She found some old bank envelopes under the car seat while she was stuck in traffic and folded them, stuffing them into the jacket of her safari pantsuit. It was chic but comfortable, and set off her nice tan. With it, she was wearing sneakers that helped her move quickly on crowded streets. She'd learned a long time ago that reporting was easier on the feet when they had a little cushioning underneath.

As she drove her small Volkswagen down back streets to city hall, she wondered if Jacob had been in town and had tried to get her but failed, since she'd been working late. She'd been so excited about that remark he'd made that she'd been crazy enough to invest in a telephone answering machine, but she knew many people would hang up rather than leave a message. She spent her free time sitting next to the telephone, staring out the window at the street below. And when she wasn't doing that, she haunted her mailbox for letters with a South Dakota postmark.

It was insane, she kept telling herself. He'd only been teasing. He hadn't really meant it. That reasoning might have convinced her except that Jacob never teased.

He had to mean it. And all her brother's well-intentioned arguments and warnings would go right out the window if Jacob ever knocked on her door. She'd follow him into burning coals if he asked her to, walk over a carpet of snakes . . . anything, because the hunger for him had grown to such monumental proportions over the long, empty years. She loved him. Anything he wanted, he could have.

She was curious about his feelings. Tom had said that Jacob didn't know what he felt for Kate. But Jacob wanted her, all right. Her innocence didn't keep her from seeing the desire in his dark eyes. It was what would happen if she made love with him that puzzled her. Would he be flattered when he knew she was a virgin? Would he even know it? They said only doctors could really tell. But he was a very experienced man—would he know?

She parked in the municipal parking lot, glancing ruefully at all the dents on the fenders of her small orange VW Beetle. They were visible in the light from the street lamps.

"Poor little thing," she said sympathetically, glaring at the big cars that surrounded it. "Don't worry, someday I'll save up enough to get your fenders smoothed out."

Someday. Maybe when she was ninety . . . Reporting, while an exciting job, was hardly the best-paid profession in the world. It exerted maximum wear and tear on nerves, emotions and body, and salary never compensated for the inevitable overtime. It was a twenty-four-hour-a-day job, and nowhere near as glamorous as television seemed to make it.

What was glamorous, she wondered as she made her way up to the alderman's offices, about covering a story on an addition to the city's sewer system? One of the meetings she'd just come from had dealt with that fascinating subject.

Alderman Barkley H. James was talking to people as reporters crowded in. People from print and broadcast media had begun setting up, most of them wearing the bland, faintly bored look that seemed to hallmark the profession. It wasn't really boredom, it was repetition. Most of these reporters were veterans, and they'd seen and heard it all. They were hard, because they had to be. That didn't mean they were devoid of emotion—just that they'd learned to pretend they didn't have it.

She slid into a seat beside Roger Dean, a reporter on a local weekly. Roger was nearer forty than thirty, a daily reporter who'd "retired" to a weekly. "Here we are again," she murmured as she checked the lighting in the office and made corrections to the settings on her 35-mm camera. "I saw you yesterday at the solid-waste-management meeting, didn't I?"

"It was a foul job, but somebody had to do it," Roger said with theatrical fervor. He glanced at her from his superior height. "Why do they always send you to those meetings?"

"When it comes to issues like sanitary-disposal sites, everybody else hides in the bathroom until Harvey picks a victim."

He shuddered. "I once covered a sanitary-landfill-site public meeting. People had guns. Knives. They yelled."

"I have survived two of those," she said with a smug grin. "At the first, there was a knock-down-drag-out fight. At the second, one man tried to throw another one out a window. I was jostled and shoved, and I still think someone pinched me in a very unpleasant way."

The alderman interrupted the conversation as he began to speak. He told of mass unemployment, of poverty below anyone's expectations. He told of living conditions that were intolerable, children playing in buildings that should have been torn down years before. Slums, he told his audience, were out of place in the twentieth century. The mayor had started the ball rolling with his excellent program of revitalization, Alderman James said. Following the mayor's example, he vowed to continue the program in this crime-stricken neighborhood.

He'd interested a group of businessmen in funding a mass renovation of the neighborhood, citing figures that showed a drop in crime corresponding directly to the upgrading of slums. He threw statistics at them rapid-fire, and outlined the plan.

When he was through, there was the usual sprint for telephones by reporters calling in stories to the rewrite desk on newspapers or to anchor people at radio and television stations. This was the culmination of a story they'd all been following closely for the past week, and that made the alderman's disclosures good copy.

Kate was almost knocked down in the stampede. She managed to find a single telephone that worked, juggled her purse for a coin, and phoned the office to give them the gist of the speech so that they'd have time to get it set up for the next edition.

She collapsed back against the wall when she was through, watching Roger come toward her slowly as if he hadn't a care in the world.

"I thought you had a computer," he said.

She glared at him. "I did. It broke. I hate machines, not to mention you weekly reporters," she muttered.

"No wild dash to the phone, no gallop back to your desk to do sidebars..."

"Ah, the calm and quiet life," he agreed with a grin. "Actually, they say weekly reporting kills more people than daily reporting. *You* don't have to paste up your copy and proof it again and do correction lines and lay them in and make up ads and answer the phone and do jobwork in the print shop behind the office and sell office supplies and take subscriptions—"

"Stop!"

He shrugged. "Just letting you know how lucky you are." He put his pen back into his shirt pocket. "Well, I'm off. Nice to see you again, Kate."

"Same here."

He glanced at her with a faint smile. "I could find time to work you in if you'd like to have dinner with me."

She was tempted. She almost said yes. He wasn't anybody's idea of Prince Charming, but she liked him and it would have been nice to talk over the frustrations of her job. "Come on, I'll buy you pizza."

She loved that. But when she thought about the unwashed dishes and unvacuumed floors and untidy bed at her apartment, her chores were too much to walk away from.

"Thanks, but I've got a mess at home that I've got to get cleaned up. Rain check?" she asked and smiled at him.

"I'd start rain for a smile like that," he said with a chuckle. "Okay. See you, pretty girl."

He winked and walked off. She stared after him, wondering how anyone in her right mind could turn down a free meal. She made her way out of the building, her thoughts full of the broken computer and of how much information from the meeting would be lost for the follow-up story she had to turn in tomorrow. Well, fortunately, she could always call and talk to the committee members. She knew them and they wouldn't mind going over the figures for her. People in political circles were some of the nicest she'd ever known.

She drove back to her apartment thinking about the new lease on life that crime-ridden neighborhood was going to get. The story she'd done for the alderman had concerned a black family of six who'd been removed from the welfare rolls without a single explanation. The father had lost his job due to layoffs, the wife had had to have a mastectomy, there were four children, all barely school age.

The father had tried to call and ask why the checks weren't coming, but the social workers had been pressed for time. Someone had put him on hold, and then he'd gone through a negative-sounding woman who'd informed him that the government didn't make mistakes; if he'd been dropped from the rolls, there was a good reason. So when Kate went to do the story, the first thing she did was to call the social agency to ask about the situation. A sympathetic social worker did some checking and dug into the case, refusing to accept the superficial information she was given. Minutes later, she called Kate back to report that a computer foul-up was responsible. The family had been confused with another family that had been found guilty of welfare violations. The error had been corrected, and now the small family was getting the temporary help it needed. That, and a lot more, because Kate's story had aroused public interest. Several prominent families had made quick contributions, and the family had been spared a grueling ordeal. But the story had haunted Kate. Society was creating more

problems than it was solving. The world, Kate philoso-
phized, was just getting too big and impersonal.

She parked her car in the basement of her apartment
building and checked to make sure her can of Mace was
within reach. It gave Kate a feeling of security when she
had to go out at night. She lived in an apartment building that had a security system, but all the same, crime was
everywhere.

It had been a long day. She wanted nothing more than
to lie down after a hot bath and just read herself into a
stupor. Even with all the difficulties, though, she had a
feeling of accomplishment, of contributing something.
God bless politicians who cared, and Chicago seemed to
be blessed with a lot of them. She wondered if the other
reporters who'd been following the story were as pleased
as she was.

The elevator was sluggish, as usual. She hit the panel
and finally it began the slow upward crawl to the fourth
floor. She got off, ambling slowly to her door. She felt
ancient.

The phone was ringing, and she listened numbly until
she realized that she'd forgotten to turn the answering
machine on. She unlocked the door and grabbed the receiver on the fourth ring.

"Hello?" she said, her voice breathless and curt. "If
that's you, Dan Harvey, try the rest room. That's where
everybody runs to hide when you need a story covered—"

"It isn't Harvey," came the reply in a deep, familiar
voice.

Her heart slammed wildly at her rib cage. "Jacob?"

She could almost hear him smiling. "I've been ringing
for the past hour. I thought you got off at five."

Her breath was sticking in her throat. She slid onto an armchair by the phone and tried to stop herself from shaking. It had been two weeks since Margo's wedding, but it felt like years. "I do," she heard herself saying. "I had to cover a story at city hall and the traffic was terrible."

"Have dinner with me," he said in a tone she'd never heard him use. "I realize it's short notice, but I didn't expect to be in town overnight."

She could have died when she remembered almost accepting Roger's offer of a meal. If she had... It didn't bear thinking about!

"It's going on six-thirty," she said, glancing at her digital clock.

"Can you be ready in thirty minutes?"

"Do birds fly?" she croaked. "Of course I can!"

He chuckled. "I'll pick you up then."

"But, wait, you don't know where I live," she said frantically.

"I know," was all he said. And the line went dead.

She looked at the receiver blankly. Well, so much for being cool and poised and keeping her head, she thought ruefully. She might as well have taken an ad in her own paper, a display ad that read: I'm yours, Jacob!

It took her only ten minutes to shower and blow-dry her hair, but finding the right dress took fifteen. She went through everything in her closet, dismissing one outfit as too demure, another as too brassy, and still another as dull and disgustingly old. The only thing left was a silky black dress with no sleeves and a deeply slit bodice that laced up. It was midknee, just a cocktail dress, but she liked its sophistication. She wore the garment with black velvet pumps and a glittering rhinestone necklace. And even if she did say so herself, she looked sharp. She left her hair long, letting it fall naturally around her shoulders like black satin, and she didn't wear much makeup. Jacob didn't like cosmetics.

He was prompt. The buzzer rang at precisely seven o'clock, and with trembling hands she pushed the button that would unlock the front door of the apartment building.

Minutes later, he was at the door. She opened it, shaking all over, while she tried to pretend that she was poised. And there he was, resplendent in a black dinner jacket and trousers, with a pleated white shirt and elegant black tie, the polish on his shoes glossy enough to reflect the carpet.

"Nice," he murmured, taking in the black dress. "I'm glad you didn't want a fast-food hamburger."

She flushed. It sounded as though he had expected her tastes not to be simple. "I . . ."

"Get your purse and let's go," he said tersely. "I've booked a table for seven-thirty."

She didn't argue. She felt on the sofa for her purse, locked the door behind her and followed him into the elevator.

"You didn't say what to wear," she faltered, stopping short of admitting that she'd dressed to the teeth just to please him, not because she expected to go anywhere fancy.

He leaned against the rail inside the elevator and stared down at her with easy sophistication. He looked like a predator tonight, and she realized with a start that she'd never been alone with him before. It was an entirely new kind of relationship, being a woman in his eyes. Everything was different suddenly, and her heart was beating like thunder.

"You're nervous around me," he said finally. "Why?"

Her slender shoulders rose and fell. "I always have been," she said quietly. "You're very intimidating."

"You're not a child anymore," he replied, his dark eyes narrowing in that bronzed face. "For tonight, you're my date, not Margo's best friend. I don't expect to have to quote etiquette or tie a bib on you."

He was being frankly insulting now, and she felt her pride reassert itself. "If you'd rather go alone...?"

He glared at her. "I might wish I had, if you don't stop this shrinking-violet act. If I'd wanted a shy little virgin, I'd have found one."

But she was! She almost told him so, too, and then she realized that it might ruin her whole evening. For years she'd wanted to be with him, to have one magical night to live on. And here she was about to send it up in smoke.

She managed a smile for him, hoping it was coquettish enough. "Sorry," she said. "It's been a long day."

He accepted her excuse after a cursory appraisal. They got off the elevator and he took her arm to lead her to his car. He'd rented a Mercedes, silvery and elegant.

"It's like yours," she said slowly as he helped her into the car. The Cade family had two cars—a black Lincoln and a silver Mercedes—as well as other ranch vehicles.

"It *is* mine," he corrected her. "You know I hate airplanes. I drove here."

"It must have taken all day," she faltered.

He got in beside her. "Two days," he said. "But that was because I stopped in Wisconsin. I had some business with a dairy farmer there."

Knowing how Jacob drove, she was surprised that he'd made it to Chicago alive. She peeked at him. "No speeding tickets?"

His eyebrows arched. "I beg your pardon?" he asked coolly.

She stared at the purse in her lap. "How many cars was it you wrecked during college?"

"I am not a bad driver," he replied arrogantly. He moved out into the traffic, barely missing a passing car. The driver sat down on his horn and Jacob glared at him. "Idiots," he muttered. "Nobody in this city can drive worth beans. I've had five close calls tonight already, just like that one."

Kate was trying not to double over laughing. It wouldn't do, it really wouldn't.

"And it wasn't three cars," he added. "It was two."

She glanced up to find a frankly amused gleam in his dark eyes. She smiled at him in spite of herself, marveling at the way the motion drew his eyes briefly to her lips.

"Who did you think I was when you answered the phone?" he asked carelessly.

"My city editor," she told him. "I get stuck with all the terrible assignments because the other reporters hide out when he wants a victim."

"You mentioned you were out covering a story," he recalled, pausing at a traffic light. He drew a cigarette from the pack in the glove compartment and lit it lazily. "What was it?"

She told him, outlining the alderman's plan for the neighborhood and the mayor's successful program of revitalization in problem areas of the city. "Cities seem pretty impersonal, and then something like this happens. It makes me feel better about urban areas," she said with a smile. "I like Chicago."

He glanced at her curiously, but he didn't say anything.

Her eyes sought his dark face, noticing how handsome he looked as the colorful city lights played over his features. "You've never asked me out before. In fact," she said softly, "I used to think that you hated me."

He pulled the car into a vacant space in front of a plush downtown restaurant, cut the engine and turned to look at her, his dark eyes steady and faintly glimmering. "Hate and desire are different sides of the same coin," he said quietly. "I couldn't very well seduce my niece's best friend."

Her heart went wild. "I...didn't realize," she faltered.

"I made damned sure you didn't realize," he said softly, watching her intently. "I've tried to protect Margo. That's why I never brought women home. You were a tough proposition, anyway—the first woman I ever wanted who was completely off-limits."

He said *wanted*, not *loved*. She had to remember to make the distinction as Tom had warned. Careful, girl, she told herself, don't let him get under your skin.

The trouble was, he was already there, very deep. She loved him too much.

"But now Margo's married," he said softly, reaching out to stroke a long strand of black hair in a way that made her body ache. "And I don't have to hide it anymore. You're almost twenty-five. You're a responsible, independent woman and you live in the city. I don't have to handle you with kid gloves, do I, Kate?"

She didn't mind how he handled her. That was the whole problem. Part of her wanted to clear up his misconceptions, to tell him about her childhood, about her very strict upbringing. But another part of her was afraid that if she told him the truth he'd hightail it back to South Dakota and never come near her again. And so she bit her tongue to keep from denying what he'd said.

He finished his cigarette leisurely, leaning forward to stub it out. The movement brought him so close to Kate that she could see the thickness of his black eyelashes, the tiny wrinkles at the corners of his eyes. She could smell the expensive cologne he wore and the fainter tang of the soap and shampoo he used.

He turned before he leaned back, catching her eyes. It was the closest she'd ever been to him. Her heart felt as if it were going to burst when he put one lean hand at her cheek and began to slowly, sensuously rub his thumb over her soft lips.

"You don't wear layers of makeup," he said softly. "I like that. And you dress like a lady." His gaze went down to the laces of her bodice, lingering there before moving up again to meet her eyes. "Are you wearing anything under that witchy dress?"

It was too intimate a question. She averted her face, trying not to look like the gauche innocent she was. "Why don't you feed me?"

He laughed softly. "All right. We'll do it your way."

Do what? She didn't even ask; it was safer not to know the answer.

The restaurant was crowded, but they had a nice table on the upper level of an interior that featured exquisite crystal chandeliers and an atmosphere of affluence that made Kate feel frumpy even in the expensive dress she was wearing. She'd had to save money for weeks to afford it; most of the other women who were sitting around this restaurant looked as if they could lay down cash for a Mercedes.

"Don't look so intimidated," Jacob mused as they were seated. "They're just people."

She laughed nervously. "If you knew how I grew up..." she began.

"I do. I've seen your grandmother Walker's house," he replied easily. "It was an old Victorian, but still elegant in its way."

"I grew up," she repeated, "in Nebraska. On a farm. My father was—" She almost said "a lay minister," but she changed it to "—poor. My mother left when Tom and I were just babies. Dad kept us until his death." Of a brain tumor, she could have added, one that made him crazy. She shuddered a little at the painful memories. After all these years, she still had a very real fear of male domination. She could hear her father shouting, feel the whip of the belt across her bare legs whenever she triggered his explosive, unpredictable temper.

"I grew up rich," Jacob replied. "We inherited money from my great-grandfather. He made a fortune back in the late 1880s, when a blizzard drove out half the cattlemen in the West. The old devil had a knack for predicting bad weather. He managed to get his cattle east before that devastating snowfall. He made a fortune."

"Money seems to bring its own responsibilities," she remarked, studying his hard, lined face and cool, dark eyes. "You never seem to have any time to yourself."

A corner of his mouth tugged up. "Don't I?"

She looked down at the white linen tablecloth. Piped music was playing around them, very romantic, while white-coated waiters tended to the crowded tables. "Not during the day, at least," she said, qualifying her words. "When Margo and I were girls, you were always being hounded by somebody."

He was watching her, his gaze purely possessive. "It goes with any kind of business, Kate. I'd hate a life of leisure."

He probably would. He didn't keep his body that fit and muscular by sitting behind a desk.

"I guess I would, too," she mused. Her slender fingers touched the heavy silver knife of her place setting. "Sometimes my job gets unpleasant, but there are compensations."

"I suppose there would be. You work with a lot of men, don't you?" he asked.

There was an unflattering double meaning in his words. She looked directly into his searching eyes, trying not to be affected by the increase in her pulse from his magnetism. "Yes," she said. "I work with a lot of men. Not just at the office, but in politics, rescue work, police work—and in all those places, I'm just one of the boys."

His gaze dropped to her bodice. "So I see."

"I don't work in suggestive clothing," she fired back. "I don't make eyes at married men, and if you're going to start making veiled remarks about what you saw in the bathhouse six years ago, I'm leaving this minute!"

"Sit down."

His tone was like ice, his eyes frankly intimidating. The cold note in his voice made her feel sick inside. She sat down, shaking a little with reaction.

"I know what it looked like to you," she said half under her breath, coloring as she realized the interest she'd raised in other diners, who glanced at the dark man and the pretty woman obviously having a lover's quarrel. "But it wasn't what you thought."

"What I saw was obvious," he returned. He stubbed out the cigarette with a vicious motion. "Gerald was damned lucky. If it had been my niece, even if she'd invited it, I'd have broken him like a toothpick."

That was in character. He fought like a tiger for his own. But not for Kate. He thought that she was little more than a tramp and that she didn't need any protection. It surprised Kate sometimes that he was so willing to believe the worst about her, when everything pointed to the contrary. He'd known her for years and he'd been so kind to her. And then, in one afternoon, he'd done an about-face in his attitude toward her. She'd never understood why.

"Lucky Margo, having you to spoil her," she said, with a wealth of pain in the words. She stared at her lap. "Tom and I never had that problem."

"Your grandmother wasn't poor," he argued.

She clenched her teeth. "I didn't mean money." It was love she and Tom had lacked. Grandmother Walker, not a demonstrative person, had never made any concessions in her way of life for them. She'd demanded that they grow up without frills or the handicap of spoiling.

He paused while the waiter brought menus. Kate studied hers with no enthusiasm at all. He'd killed her appetite stone dead.

"What do you want?" he asked carelessly.

She glanced up at him with a speaking look, and he actually laughed.

"Talk about looks that could kill," he murmured. "Were you wishing I was on the menu?"

"I hate you," she said, and meant it. "The biggest mistake I've made in years was to agree to come out with you at all. No, I don't want anything on the menu. I'd like to leave. You stay and enjoy your meal, and I'll get a cab—"

"That isn't all you'll get if you don't sit down, Kate," he replied quietly. "I hate scenes."

"I've never made one in my life until tonight," she said shortly. Her green eyes were huge in her ashen face as she stared across the table at him. How could he treat her this way when she loved him to distraction?

He stared at her with a mingling of emotions, the strongest of which was desire. She was, he thought, the most delicious tidbit he'd ever seen. He'd spent years chiding himself for his unbridled passion for her. Now the barriers were down, and he couldn't seem to handle the confusion she aroused in him. God, she was lovely! All his secret dreams of perfection, hauntingly sweet and seductive. He wondered how many other men had wanted her, had been with her, and the strength of his jealousy disturbed him. It didn't matter, he told himself, he had to have her. Just once, he told himself. Just once, to know that soft, sweet body in passion. Then the fever would be gone. He'd be free of her spell.

She couldn't know that he'd suddenly seen her as a woman when she'd kissed that boy so hungrily. It had gotten worse when he'd confronted them in the bath-house, and the desire he'd felt for her had almost knocked him to his knees.

He hadn't even meant to take her out tonight. But the lure of her was irresistible. He couldn't stop. And it wasn't bad that she was experienced; he was even glad, in a way, because he had too many scruples about seduc-ing innocents. If he made love to a virgin, he'd feel an obligation to marry her. It wasn't a modern outlook, but then he wasn't a modern man. He was country bred and raised, for all his money.

She looked sad, he thought, studying her. His own emotions confused and irritated him. He wanted her un-til she was a living obsession in his mind. He ached all over already, and he hadn't even touched her. His dark eyes narrowed, studying her. She was lovely, all right. A walking, breathing temptation. Yes, it was just as well that she wasn't innocent. If he didn't believe her to be sophisticated, he'd never be able to seduce her.

He leaned back in his chair and let his eyes wander over her bodice, where bare skin peeked through the lacing. "Look at me."

She stared back at him with trembling lips, almost shaking with fury. He'd ruined it. All her beautiful dreams had crumbled. Her voice choked when she spoke. "I shouldn't have come with you. Roger Dean offered me a nice pizza. I should have settled for that."

His chin lifted. "Roger who?"

"Roger Dean," she shot back, gratified that he looked irritated. "He's a reporter for one of the other papers. A handsome and very nice man," she added. "And he likes me just the way I am."

So she did have other men. That touched something vulnerable inside him and hurt it. Unsmiling, he stared at her. "Did you turn down a date with him to come out with me?" he asked, as if he expected she did things like that often.

"I turned him down before you called," she shot back. "Sorry to shatter your black image of me."

He sighed deeply and paused long enough to give the waiter an order for steak and a baked potato.

"What do you want?" he asked Kate politely.

"I'll have a shrimp cocktail and coffee," she murmured.

"You need more than that," Jacob said.

"That's all I want, thank you." She gave the waiter the menu with a wan smile, and Jacob noticed how worn she looked, how tired. He knew suddenly that it was a sense of excitement gone sour.

"I've spoiled the night for you, haven't I?" he asked with sharp perception, lighting a cigarette as he studied her.

Her lips curved into a rueful smile. "I broke speed records getting ready," she said. "Went through every dress I had in my wardrobe to find something nice enough to wear for you. I suppose I was a little excited, being asked out by you after all these years, when I thought I was more of a pest and irritation than some-one you ... wanted to date." Her eyes glanced off the expression of frank surprise in his. "I should have re-membered how you feel about me. It's my own fault. Nobody held a gun on me."

He put out his cigarette slowly, his heart doing odd things inside his chest at that confession. He hadn't thought she might want to be with him. At times he'd wondered if she might feel a little of the physical attrac-tion for him that he felt for her. But Kate was mysteri-ous. She was close-lipped and very private, in spite of her modern outlook.

"Maybe we could bury the hatchet for once," he murmured, feeling this way for the first time in his life. The self-confidence he'd always had with women was lacking tonight. He felt something new with Kate, and everything in him was fighting it. She confused him, dis-turbed him. She had to be sophisticated, but why did she sound so damned honest? She'd sworn once that she'd never lied to him, and he'd had to fight not to believe her. He couldn't believe her, because if he did ... He stared at her, feeling something tingle inside him as her face col-ored. He couldn't prevent a warm, quiet smile.

His smile could open doors. She stared at him with wonder. He'd never smiled at her like that. She returned his smile with interest. "Perhaps we could," she said, her voice husky.

He reached across the table and found her hand, lift-ing it in his to study it. No rings of any kind. A slender, graceful hand with neatly rounded fingernails, no trace of polish on them. He frowned a little. Touching her made his breath come quickly.

Kate's breath caught as he rubbed his thumb slowly over her palm, whipping up sweet storms of emotion. He looked up into her eyes, holding them, searching them, in a silence that whirled away the other diners and the whole world.

His fingers gripped hers with sudden passion, his face hardened, his breathing stopped in his throat. "Kate," he whispered roughly, and his fingers began to work their way between hers in an act as intimate as kissing. He had sensitive hands, very lean, darkly tanned and strong from hours of working cattle, fixing equipment, doing all the things that ranch work required even of the boss.

Her hand trembled as his eyes held hers in a contact that was as arousing as the slow, exquisite tracing of his fingers between hers. She felt her breath quickening, her body reacting to the newness of it all.

"Years," Jacob whispered roughly, his dark eyes blazing into hers as his body caught fire with the electric contact. "I've waited years for tonight, Kate."

Did he mean…could he mean…? She swallowed down a burst of excited confessions and bit her tongue. She had to take it slowly—she couldn't blurt out undying love and ruin everything. She looked at their joined hands, hers so pale in his dark, strong one. She'd waited years, too, and tonight was the reality after the golden dream. But was his dream the same as hers? Had they been waiting for the same reason?

Four

The waiter brought food and broke the spell. Kate went through the motions of eating, but her mind was on the wondrous emotions she was feeling with Jacob. He was content now to discuss general subjects, nothing intimate. But underneath it all, she suspected that he was still as disturbed physically as she was. His eyes were much darker than usual, and he hardly took them off her.

He finished his steak and leaned back to light a cigarette. "Want dessert?" he asked gently.

She was excited by that note in his voice. It was tender, and openly warm. "No," she said. "I don't really like sweets."

He chuckled. "Neither do I, although I'm partial to an apple cake. Janet, our housekeeper, bakes one occasionally when my father asks nicely."

"Your father is a nice man," she said quietly.

"Nice. That about sums it up. No one, ever, could accuse me of being . . . nice," he added with a cool look.

"We can't all be fiery and hard," she reminded him.

"If I hadn't been, we'd have lost Warlance twelve years ago," he said shortly. "There is such a thing as common sense. My father was spending capital faster than the ranch was making it. Ranching has seen hard times in past years. Every year, more ranchers go bust."

"You never will," she muttered.

"I'm not superhuman," he replied surprisingly, "and I've made some bad mistakes. But a soft attitude gets you nowhere in business. My father should have been an inventor. He'd rather putter around in his workshop than talk cattle futures."

She searched his face. "Your mother wasn't a dreamer, was she?" she asked softly, daringly.

His dark eyes seemed to blaze up for an instant. He stared at his cigarette. "I hated her," he said half under his breath. "From the day I was old enough to understand what she was doing to my father, I hated her. She was nothing but a tramp, with an eye out to opportunity. She sent for me once, after she married that Texan, and I went. It was almost amusing, watching her try to explain."

"You didn't even listen, did you?" she asked sadly.

His eyes grew cold. "You can't imagine what my childhood was like."

Yes, she could understand, she thought. With his black pride, it must have been pure hell. "You went away to school eventually, didn't you?"

"Dad got tired of being called into the principal's office twice a week," he replied, lifting the cigarette to his mouth. "I was in scraps constantly."

She searched his hard face. "My father said that my mother was like that." She spoke hesitantly, her voice soft and unsteady. He looked up, curious. "I never knew her, you see. And my father was very sick and his mind came and went. But he seemed to always be afraid that I was going to be like her."

He had to bite his tongue almost through to keep the sarcastic words from pouring out. Wasn't she like that? He frowned at her bitter expression, amazed at his own lack of sensitivity. What was it about Kate that made him doubt every word she said? Why was it so impossible for him to trust her?

"I made sure that Margo knew right from wrong," he commented. "I didn't browbeat her, but I got my point across. So did my father." He put out his cigarette. He didn't want to hear about Kate's childhood, or know any more about her than he already did. He didn't know why, either. What he felt for her was only desire, surely. And every time he looked at her, that got worse.

"Are you ready to go?" he asked.

"Yes. Of course."

She watched him pay the check, feeling numb. She'd bored him, and now he was going to take her home and go back to South Dakota. It might be months before she saw him again. Or she might never see him again. He didn't seem to like her any better now than he had before. His attitude was even colder, in a way.

He took her arm and led her out into the silky night, into the sounds of traffic and the bright lights. "I'd never get used to living in the city," he remarked as he helped her into the Mercedes and then moved to the driver's side. "I like wide spaces too much," he told her as he got in the car.

"I couldn't sleep for a long time when I first moved here," she said with a soft smile. "The sirens and horns kept me awake. It's a far cry from howling dogs and lowing cattle."

"Yes."

She watched his face as he started the car and pulled away from the restaurant. Well, why deny herself that pleasure, she asked bitterly, when he'd be gone in a few minutes and it would be the first and last time she'd be alone with him.

He stopped at a traffic light and turned his head just a fraction of an inch to look at her. His dark eyes searched hers.

"You're staring," he said bluntly.

"I know," she replied, her voice soft and full of dreams.

He reached out and caught her hand, bringing it to his hard thigh. He held it there as he drove, letting her feel the ripple of muscle as he eased up and down on the accelerator, his fingers linked into hers, caressing.

By the time they reached her apartment house, his nerves were stripped and raw. He cut off the engine and turned to her, releasing her hand slowly. She was still watching his face, shadowed under the streetlight, and his heart was beating wildly with a kind of hunger that challenged every ounce of control he had.

Kate felt her pride falling away. She loved him so much. What comfort was pride when, after he left, she'd be alone for the rest of her life?

"Oh, Jacob, kiss me," she whispered, pleaded, her shy hands touching his, faintly tremulous. "Just once—!"

The words drove him crazy. He reached for her, much too roughly, but his body was on fire. He turned her face up to his, feeling fiercely male, possessive. His breath came harshly as he looked down into her hungry eyes.

"Open your mouth and put it against mine, Kathryn," he whispered huskily, drawing her face up to his.

The words thrilled as much as those hard, warm hands on her cheeks. It had been the secret longing of her life. To kiss him . . .

Her eyes closed on stinging tears as she obeyed him. For years she'd dreamed of this, ached for it, prayed for it. It was happening. She could feel the hard, smoky warmth of his lips as she fitted hers slowly to them, trembling a little with the sudden freedom of being allowed to love him, to express all she felt physically.

"Jacob," she breathed brokenly, sliding her hands against his shirtfront, inside the jacket which he'd unbuttoned when they'd climbed into the car. She could feel hard muscle and something springy, like hair, under the soft fabric. She moved closer, pushing upward against his mouth in aching hunger.

He eased her head against his shoulder as he slowly increased the pressure of his mouth, opening her lips fully to the sudden moist penetration of his tongue. Even in that, he was delicate, teasing before he took possession, guiding her into an intimacy that was overwhelming in its sweet pleasure.

Her fingers were still stroking over his breastbone, and she felt his hand move over them, shifting them, while he flicked the buttons open.

He put her hand into the small opening he'd made, spreading the palm over thick hair and moving it sensuously back and forth to show her the motion he liked.

The hunger grew suddenly, like a flash flood on the desert. One minute he was delicately teasing, the next, he was crushing her back against the seat and his mouth was fiercely demanding. Kate gave without reservation, in heaven at the tempestuous ardor that outmatched even her dreams. She began to moan softly, unaware of the sudden, unbearable desire that was coiling in the body of the man above her.

He drew back, his breathing faintly unsteady, his heart like a drum under her hand.

"We can't sit down here doing this all night," he whispered. His dark eyes searched her shadowed ones. "Do we go to your apartment or my hotel room? Or do I go home alone?"

It should have been the latter. She should have told him that she was a virgin, that he was asking something of her that he had no right to ask, especially considering his treatment of her. But maybe he wouldn't know. She'd been alone all her life. Wasn't she entitled to one bright memory in all that darkness? To one sweet hour in a man's arms, pretending that he loved her as much as she loved him? Surely, loving gave her that right.

"Don't . . . go home," she whispered.

He searched her eyes for a long moment, hiding the sweet triumph he felt at her capitulation while he tried not to wonder if she always gave in so easily to a man.

He released her and got out, opening her door for her. They went up to her apartment in a stoic silence. She felt uneasy, and the feeling got worse as she opened her apartment and let him inside.

She turned to tell him that she wasn't sure, to explain about her past. But he turned her, very slowly, expertly, so that her back was against the door. And he bent, his mouth breathing on hers, into hers, as his lips formed the very shape of her mouth and teased it.

In the soft, semidark silence of her apartment, with the outside sounds of sirens and horns fading into nothing, she felt his hands at her hips. And then his body was easing down completely on hers, pressing her back against the steely cold of the door. She felt the hardness of his body and knew instinctively what was happening to him. Her own body reacted to it in a way she'd never expected, by arching gently to press up against his hips, to encourage his ardor.

He trailed his fingers from her hip to her thigh and back up again, coaxing her to repeat the involuntary movement. And all the while, his mouth was growing more intimate with hers, tasting her in a new, tender way.

He shifted her just a little and she felt his hand at the laces that held her bodice together.

She trembled at the newness of what he was doing, a little shocked at the feel of his hands touching her there. Her eyes opened, big and curious. That amused him, because he was certain that he wasn't the first man to touch her. But she was hungry for him, and that was satisfying.

He had the last of the laces undone now, and he started to push the fabric away from her full, soft breasts, when her hand instinctively caught his wrist in a token protest.

"Don't pretend, Kate," he said softly. "I told you before, I don't want anything to do with a virgin."

That meant that he was going to walk out the door and never come back if she admitted that she was innocent. She bit her lip worriedly. Would he know when he had her in bed? Could men tell, especially experienced men? He'd be furious....

"What a look," he murmured, bending to her soft mouth. "Stop biting that lip," he whispered. "Bite mine instead."

He nibbled at her, arousing new and unexpected twinges of pleasure. She caught at his shirt when he began again to push the fabric away and she felt his fingers tracing around the edges of her breast.

"Relax," he breathed, feeling her tremble. "We've got all night. There's no hurry."

But there was, because she was frightened of having him find out the truth. She loved him. She wanted nothing more out of life than to give him a night that would haunt him all his life.

She wasn't experienced, but she was a great reader. She knew a lot about men that came from wildly romantic books, and now she drew on it.

Her hands went into his shirt, her nails drawing through that thick dark hair to the warm skin underneath. Her hips arched in a slow rhythm against his, brushing his thighs sensuously.

He shuddered, and the mouth over hers grew rough. His hand stopped its teasing and swallowed her breast whole, his palm rubbing against the hard nipple, his fingers contracting.

She felt him tremble faintly, and knew a wild fever of exultation. He was so aroused that he was losing control. She could feel it, taste it, in the sudden roughness of passion she'd aroused in him. He shifted, lowering his body, one knee forcing its way between her thighs. He removed his hand from her breast and, still holding her mouth under his, stripped her to the waist. Then he was against her, his hard chest against her soft breasts, his hips against hers with a sudden intimacy that dragged a shattering cry from her throat.

She was on fire for him. His hands were on her skin now, touching her in ways she'd never dreamed a man would ever touch her. He managed to undress them both while they stood there, her mind in such a fever of tension and hunger that it was an actual relief to have his hard, warm body against hers with no barriers to the beauty of shared nudity.

His mouth was demanding, insistent, as he lifted her, finally, and carried her into the bedroom. He had barely taken time to whip off the coverlet when his body was over hers, his mouth burning on her skin as he explored every single inch of her.

By the time she felt him position her, she was trembling all over, her eyes blurred by a mist of shuddering need.

"Jacob," she moaned, tears in her eyes as she looked up into a face dark with passion, eyes so black they were almost frightening.

"Don't talk," he whispered roughly. He pinned her down, his hands locking with hers, his hips shifting over her prone body.

"Be . . . careful," she managed through lips that felt parched.

"I won't hurt you," he breathed. "Just relax."

By the time she realized what he was saying, he was already becoming part of her body. She watched his face, awed by what she saw and felt. Her hips tautened, but he brushed a gentle hand over her thighs, soothing her, his eyes burning into hers.

She shuddered. It wasn't just discomfort, it was pain. He bent then and put his mouth on hers, biting into it with shuddering hunger as his body began to move jerkily.

She pushed at his chest, but it was too late. He thought her moans were pleasure; he thought her sudden, sharp, shifting movements meant she was reaching a pinnacle. Her reaction pushed him over the edge for the first time in his life. Tears boiled from her eyes, but he didn't see. He drove for his own fulfillment, losing himself in a

frenzy of passion that exploded in a fire storm of ecstasy. He cried out with the anguished force of it, his
body racked by coiling muscles.

It was all he could do to protect her. He barely made it
at all, gasping for just enough air to breathe, his nostrils
full of the exquisite scent of her, his body resting on her
silky softness, so exhausted with pleasure that he could
have died and not minded.

A long time later, he became aware of broken sobs. He
lifted his dark, damp head and looked down into her pale
face, her eyes filled with tears.

"I hurt you?" he whispered belatedly.

She pushed at his chest. "Please..."

Her expression said it all. He rolled away, scowling.
That wasn't the look of a woman who'd been loved.
"Wait," he called as she started blindly toward the
bathroom. "For God's sake, come back here and let me
make it up to you—"

"Make it...up to me?" she whispered. "I'd rather die
than let you do that again! Oh, God, how horrible!"

She ran into the bathroom and locked the door, feeling sick to her soul at what she'd let him do. It had been
painful at first, and then he'd succeeded in making her
feel things she wanted to forget. Great throbbing surges
of pleasure that had made her feel wanton, that had made
her want to bite and claw and rake him with her nails.
And just as that pleasure had begun, he was already
through with her. The frustration had her wild, sick with
anguish. So that was sex. A woman was teased with fulfillment while a man drowned in it. It was horrible, almost to reach the sky, only to plummet down in
unsatisfied anguish. And he wanted her to go through
that again, just so that he could enjoy himself? She was

too frustrated to begin to think straight, to understand any of it. She burst into tears.

The man dressing coldly in the next room was feeling some frustrations of his own. His lovemaking had been called a few different things over the years, but horrible was a new one. His own loss of control was what hurt the most, that he'd been that vulnerable and that she knew it. He hadn't pleased her, but he hadn't realized just how far gone he was. If she'd been willing, he could have made it up to her. But the expression on her face, in her eyes, had been damning. He'd disappointed her. He'd . . . disgusted her. He zipped his trousers and shouldered furiously into his shirt. He wanted to throw things. For God's sake, didn't she realize she'd worked him into that frenzy? Why push him out of control and then complain when she didn't reach fulfillment? It was her fault. Or maybe this was some game she played with men, a cover-up for her own frigidity, something to compensate for her lack of passion. She'd been passionate at first, though. What had gone wrong?

He finished dressing and the more he thought about what she'd said, the madder he got. Horrible, was it? Well, she needn't worry, she'd never have to suffer him again in that respect. He combed his hair, glaring at his own reflection in the mirror, feeling more unsettled than he could ever remember.

Coming from the bathroom were muffled sounds that made his sense of frustration and confusion even worse.

"Open this door, or so help me, I'll break it down," he said in a voice that dared her to disobey.

She wrapped a bath sheet around her aching body and opened the door a fraction. She couldn't meet his eyes, so she only looked as high as his taut jaw.

"For services rendered," he said with a cold smile, and tucked a hundred-dollar bill in the bath sheet. "Maybe that will make up for your lack of enjoyment."

And he turned and stormed out the door, leaving her in tears of mingled disappointment and cold fury.

It didn't occur to her, because she knew nothing about men in intimate situations, that his own frustration and guilt and wounded male vanity, coupled with an unprecedented loss of control, had caused him to make that final insulting gesture. She took it at face value. All those years of loving him, wanting him, and this was how it had ended. He'd only wanted her body. He hadn't even known that she was innocent. He'd used her and then walked out without a kind word.

She bathed the scent of him from her body and pulled on a granny gown that covered her from head to toe. She stripped the bed, threw the sheets into the washing machine and went to sleep on her sofa. As she cried herself to sleep, she wondered if she'd ever be able to look at that bed again, much less sleep on it.

The next morning, what she'd done hit her right between the eyes the instant she woke up. She was a fallen woman. At least, that's what her father would have called her. It was probably what Jacob thought, too.

She got up and got dressed for work, her mind and body aching, haunted by guilt and bitterness about her own weakness. Now she was going to have to sweat it out, because despite what she imagined was his attempt to take precautions, there was still a chance that she could become pregnant.

Oddly enough, the thought of having Jacob's child, despite what he'd done to her, wasn't at all disturbing. It would be nice to have something small and sweet to protect and cuddle. It would be nice to have someone of her own. Then reality surfaced, and she could imagine herself trying to keep such an event secret from her own brother, Margo—and Jacob. If she realized the possibilities, he must, too. Despite his anger, he'd keep up with her through Tom. If she got pregnant, he'd know. And the world would end. She had no intention of being forced to marry him because of a baby. She'd run away to Africa with the Peace Corps. She'd sign on as a gunrunner. She'd... It was eight o'clock in the morning, for God's sake. She'd be late!

She got to the office just in time to be sent out on assignment to a fire. It was a small one, thank God, and no injuries occurred. But she liked the oblivion of being caught up in the dark excitement. And when she got back to the office, she went and asked the managing editor if there wasn't a slot open on the police beat.

"Sure," Morgan Winthrop told her. "But do you think you'd like that kind of thing, Kate? It's a pretty gory job."

"Let me try," she pleaded.

"Okay," he said after a minute. "It's yours."

She could have kissed him. Now she'd have something to occupy her mind, something to keep her on her toes and away from memories that would destroy her. Eventually she might have to cope with the devastation Jacob had wrought on her emotions, but not just yet.

Tom called her a week later, but she didn't tell him anything about her disastrous date with Jacob or her new assignment. He was working on a big new account at the ad agency and would be out of town for a week or so. But he was going to stop by to spend a couple of days with her on the way back, if she didn't mind. Of course not, she assured him, grateful that it wouldn't be right away. She was going to need a little time to cope with her fall from grace.

It was hectic, getting into the routine of the new job. She worked with Bud Schuman, the police reporter who'd often regaled her with tales of old Chicago. He seemed to be at least sixty years old, but she never dared ask his age. He might be ninety.

He kept a police radio with a few forbidden crystals in it that picked up channels he shouldn't have had access to.

"Now, now, it's not exactly dishonest," he told her. "It's psychic. At least, that's what I tell the police when they want to know how I found out something. That's another thing, sweet, never ask them if there's anything going on. Ask them if a particular thing is going on and if they've made an arrest. You can always check the police blotter if you have to."

It was an experience, she found, working with the veteran reporter. He seemed to know everyone at the local police precinct, as well as the civil defense people, the ambulance services personnel, the firemen and rescue workers and even most of the secretaries. He taught her little loopholes in information gathering that she'd never have suspected and ways of digging out facts that were nothing short of mystifying.

As Morgan Winthrop had warned her, it could be a gory job. There were murders and suicides and traffic fatalities. There were on-the-job accidents and people incinerated in fires. There were drowning victims and abused children and the occasional shoot-out. At times, the job was even a bit dangerous. But it gave Kate very little time to think, and that made it acceptable.

The only bad times were at night, when she was alone in her apartment. She'd accepted a date with Roger Dean just to get out and away from the ghost that haunted her, but it had been a minor disaster. She and Roger had nothing in common except reporting, and although they had enough stories to tear apart and comment on, their personal views of life were poles apart. Kate found herself thinking of Jacob when she was with Roger. It wasn't really fair to compare other men with Jacob, anyway. He was one of a kind.

She wondered if Jacob ever thought about the night he'd spent with her, or wondered afterward about her reaction to it. It must have wounded his pride to think that she'd found him "horrible," especially when she hadn't explained what she meant. But what he'd done to her was even worse. She'd kept that hundred-dollar bill as a reminder, so that she wouldn't ever again forget what kind of man he was. She should have listened to Tom's warning. He'd known from the beginning what Jacob was up to, and she hadn't. She'd thrown away all her ideals for that one magic "night to live on." And it had been a nightmare of discomfort, embarrassment and guilt. Even now, she flushed every time she thought about it. She'd even gone so far as to trade the bed for a new one, just to rid herself of the memory.

If only she could keep Jacob out of her mind. She knew him now in every way there was. How he made love. What he looked like in passion. Every inch of that magnificent body without the civilizing veneer of clothing. Her eyes closed. It had started to be so beautiful, and then her own fear of his realizing that she was a virgin had driven her to arouse him beyond his control. She wondered if that loss of control was normal. She knew so little about men. Perhaps any of them could go crazy in a woman's arms, but she hadn't expected Jacob to be so vulnerable.

The one thing she had to be thankful for was that she wasn't pregnant. She'd known only a week later that she had nothing to worry about on that score. But the guilt continued.

On the evening that Tom arrived, she'd just covered a grisly murder that had terrorist connections. An underground radical group had apparently murdered a Middle Eastern family in town and Kate wondered if she'd ever forget what she'd seen in their home. It was that kind of story that made her new job less than perfect. It was one thing to see crimes solved, but quite another to see the graphic results of them.

"You look whacked, Sis," Tom remarked over the small meal she'd prepared for them. "Hard day?"

"Harder than I can tell you," she sighed. "I've got a new beat. I think it's beating me," she added humorously.

"What are you doing now?"

"Police beat," she said in between bites. "We had a massacre today."

Tom put his fork down. "That's no job for you," he said. He searched her face. "What's happened? Something's gone wrong, hasn't it?"

She wanted to tell him, to confide in him as she had when they were children. But this was too personal, too intimate, to share even with a brother.

She dropped her green eyes to the table, ruffling her hair. She'd had it all cut off the day after her date with Jacob, another vain attempt to kill the memories. It was very short, and it gave her a sophisticated look. She was more mature now, and her eyes had a haunted look that added to it.

"I'm all right," she said.

"Are you in trouble?" he asked bluntly.

She bit her lower lip. "No."

"I didn't mean that kind of trouble," he said with an amused smile. "You're not the liberated kind. You'd never sleep with a man without marriage."

Boy, was he in for a shock. She studied her fingernails. "Well, Tom, actually—"

The sudden jangling of the phone made her jump. She got up and went to answer it, her heart running away. Every time it rang, she expected it to be Jacob, God knew why. It never was, of course. It never would be.

She lifted it. "Hello?"

"It's Bud," her co-worker said abruptly. "I've just fallen down the steps and twisted my damned ankle. I can't walk. The police have cornered that bunch that killed the family." He gave her the address, which she scribbled down on a piece of paper. "Got your camera? Harvey may send a photographer, but there was nobody on the place when I left. Get going, girl, you may get an exclusive! I was tipped off!"

"You bet!" she told him. "I'm on my way."

She hung up, her eyes unnaturally bright as she searched for her camera and checked to see that the flash whined on when she keyed it, and that she had film in the camera. "I've got to run out for a few minutes," she told Tom, who was watching her curiously. "The police have nabbed the gang that killed that family I told you about. I'll be back as soon as I can."

"I don't like this," Tom said curtly. "And there's something I have to tell you. I didn't just happen along by accident. Jacob asked me to come."

She gaped at him, her face going white, her eyes huge. "Jacob?" she whispered.

He frowned. "What the hell's going on?" he demanded. "He wasn't even coherent. Well, he was, but he

kept saying something about making a decision and that
he wanted to talk to you, but he knew you wouldn't open
the door to him if I didn't come."

She stared wildly around. "Jacob—coming here?" she
asked in a choking tone.

"Yes. Tonight. That's what I was leading up to—" he
began again.

"I have to go." Her hands trembled. She clutched the
camera and grabbed up her purse. "I'll be back when I
can."

"Can't someone else do this for you?" he asked helplessly.

"No. Goodbye, Tom." She glanced at him from the
door, her face ashen, and then she was gone, a blur of
jeans and jacket.

It wasn't fifteen minutes later that Jacob arrived. Tom
let him into the apartment, his eyes haunted, his face
drawn. Jacob didn't look much better.

"She isn't here," Tom told the older man. "There's
some kind of police bust going on. She's down there with
a camera getting the story."

Jacob stuck a cigarette in his mouth and glared at Tom.
"She was doing politics, wasn't she? What in hell is she
doing covering police news?"

Tom watched him closely from his armchair. "That's
what I wanted to know. She wouldn't tell me."

Jacob went to the window, restless and oddly hesi-
tant. He opened the curtain and stared out, his tan suit
straining against hard muscle. "No, I guess she
wouldn't," he said.

"It's none of my business," Tom began, watching the
taller man. "But there's something you need to know
about Kate. I don't think you'd be cold-blooded enough
to seduce her, but there are things you have to under-

stand, just in case the thought crosses your mind. So I'm going to tell you about it. Our father was a lay minister."

The broad back stiffened. The face Tom couldn't see had gone a pasty white. "Was he?"

"He had a brain tumor. Our mother left when we were young, because she had the misfortune to fall in love with another man. There was no affair. She divorced our father before she remarried, but he got custody because of his religious affiliation. The court didn't know, you see, that he was crazier than a bedbug."

Jacob had turned, the cigarette forgotten in his hand. He stared at Tom without speaking.

Tom got up, stuck his hands in his pockets and paced. "He drummed morality into us until Kate and I were terrified of sex. He made it into something incredibly bad. His mind was going, of course. He loved our mother and she'd betrayed him. All that worked toward making him worse. In the end, Kate smiled at a boy at a supermarket, and our father beat her right there in public with a belt. It took three men to stop him, and he went into convulsions. He died right there."

Jacob sat down heavily in a chair, his eyes wild.

Tom stood over him. "Kate should have told you. I had to, in case you've got some half-baked idea of seducing her. She's so much in love with you that she just might give in. But afterward ... She's carrying so many scars from childhood, I don't know what she might do."

"In ... love with me?" Jacob was ash white.

"Don't tell me you didn't know?" Tom shook his head. "Honest to God, Jacob, everybody knows. There's never been a man in Kate's life except you. She's got pictures of you that she begged from Margo hidden all over the apartment. I'll bet money there's one even here—

aha.'' He opened the drawer in a small table by Jacob and produced a dog-eared photograph of Jacob on a horse, one that Margo had taken years ago.

Jacob put his head in his hands. He felt sick to his soul. "She's a virgin, isn't she," he said dully, stating it, not even asking.

"She and I both are," Tom said without embarrassment. "Those kinds of scars are hard to get rid of. I expect I'll marry someday, regardless. But it will take one hell of a woman to accept me the way I am. It'll take one hell of a man to accept Kate.''

Jacob wanted to jump out the window. He couldn't remember a time in his life when he ever felt suicidal, but he felt that way now. He remembered Kate's odd reluctance to be touched, and then her reaction to him, her final words. Of course he'd hurt her, and he'd made it worse...that hundred-dollar bill.

He stood up, his face like rice paper, his eyes blazing. "Oh, my God," he breathed. He looked at Tom. "My God, why didn't you tell me?''

Tom frowned slightly. "You seemed to dislike her..." he began.

"Dislike her." Jacob's voice was haunted, his eyes as dead as winter leaves. "I'd have walked over fire to get to her. But I couldn't let her see how I felt. A man can't give a woman that kind of hold on him, Tom!''

Tom stared at him blankly. It was all such a puzzle. Kate's distraught attitude, Jacob's shock at learning the truth. What was going on?

The buzz for the front door downstairs was as loud as a bomb in the silence of the apartment. No one could get into the apartment building unless the person in the apartment they wanted to visit pushed a button to open the outside door. Tom and Jacob exchanged glances.

"Maybe she forgot her key," Tom said. He pressed the button. "Yes?"

"Police," came the terse reply. "Is there a Tom Walker here?"

Tom glanced at Jacob, his face a study in fear. "Yes. I'm Tom Walker. Come on up." He pressed the button.

Jacob put out his cigarette with a hand that trembled. He didn't know how he was going to live with what he'd learned tonight. And if something had happened to Kate, before he had time to try and make it up to her...

Tom opened the door on the first knock. A tall, uniformed man stood there. The expression on his face spoke volumes.

"It's my sister, Kate, isn't it?" Tom asked with terror in his voice.

The man nodded. "There was a shoot-out when the terrorists made a break for it. One of the men had an Uzi automatic. Kate was behind a sign. The bullets penetrated. We had her taken to the hospital."

"She's still alive?" Jacob asked from behind Tom, his voice odd.

"She was when the ambulance left," the policeman continued. He searched Tom's white face. "I'm sorry. I think it was a gut wound."

Tom stared at him blankly, but Jacob didn't. His hands were clenched at his side and he exchanged a look with the policeman that was all too knowing.

"I'll drive you to the hospital," Jacob said quietly.

"Yes...if you would." Tom turned to thank the policeman.

"I've only known young Kate for two years," the grizzled veteran said. "But she's quite a girl. If you tell her something in confidence, she'll keep it to herself. Not a lot of people in any profession can do that—especially reporters. I'm sorry. I liked her."

He nodded and left them to follow.

"Why put it like that?" Tom growled as Jacob locked the door behind them, his heart like lead in a body that had gone numb with shock. "Why use the past tense?"

"You don't know what a gut wound means," Jacob said dully. "I do."

Tom looked at him and seemed to go even paler. "No," he whispered. "Oh, no."

"Maybe he was mistaken," Jacob said. His hopes lifted faintly at the thought. "Let's go and see."

"If you know how to pray, we might try that," Tom murmured.

Try it? Jacob hadn't stopped since the ordeal began. He led the younger man down to the elevator, thinking blindly that if Kate died, he didn't want to go on living. The thought was as shocking as what had happened to her.

Five

Kate was just going into surgery by the time Tom and Jacob got to the hospital. Tom thought privately that they might have done better to take a cab. Jacob's driving was none too confidence inspiring even on good days, and the older man had almost wrecked the car twice getting there. Nothing showed on that impassive face, but Jacob's eyes were terrible to look into. For a man who had vowed never to let any woman get a hold on him, Jacob looked for all the world as if Kate had a good grip.

Tom went to the emergency desk to ask for news while Jacob sat numbly on a vinyl-covered sofa and pulled an ashtray closer on the magazine-littered table that faced it. The waiting room was filled full with ragged-looking young men, and a few babies crying miserably while their mothers shifted them and looked resigned and worn. Jacob glanced at one of the babies, a chubby little one with a smile on its face, and found himself smiling tenderly at it. He'd always thought that one day he'd have a child, but he'd never been able to commit himself to marry anyone. And then it occurred to him that he might have made Kate pregnant.

He'd tried to protect her, but it was a halfhearted measure at best. It suddenly occurred to him that if he had given her a baby, he might have cost two lives with his misguided desire. He got up abruptly, a smoking cigarette in his hand, and stared toward Tom.

The younger man was talking to a man in green cotton pants and shirt. The older man looked grave and shrugged when Tom asked a somber question. He patted Tom on the shoulder, smiled reassuringly and walked away.

"Well?" Jacob asked quickly, his eyes dark and haunted.

"That was the surgeon," Tom mumbled. He leaned against the cold wall and stared ahead at the opposite wall. His eyes were wet. "They're going to do an emergency exploratory to see how much damage the bullet did. We won't know anything for about an hour."

"How is she?" Jacob's dark eyes narrowed with worry.

"In pain," Tom replied tersely. "It hit a rib and punctured her lung. The lung collapsed."

"Poor little thing," Jacob said, closing his eyes.

"I feel sick all over," Tom said blankly. "Jacob, she's all I've got."

Jacob stared at him. "What about the man who did it?"

"Two of the terrorists were killed, the rest are in custody. It could have been any one of them. Nobody knows." He folded his arms across his chest and sighed restlessly. "I still don't understand how it happened.

Kate's never been interested in doing police news. She hates that sort of thing, but apparently she requested the job.''

Jacob turned away, his face expressionless, and took a draw from his cigarette. He knew why she'd taken the job, all right. Kate had been looking, consciously or subconsciously, for a way out, an escape from the guilt she surely must have felt. Her sense of anguish had been compounded by his own callous treatment of her. That hundred-dollar bill was going to haunt him for the rest of his life, whether she lived or died. He'd never felt so sick or frightened, and there was absolutely nothing he could do.

A balding older man with a cane hobbled toward them, pale and anxious. He went right past Tom and Jacob to the information clerk. "Kate Walker," he began breathlessly, "how is she? Do they know anything yet?"

Tom and Jacob glanced at him. "That must be the reporter whose place she took," Tom began. "He hurt his ankle—"

Jacob's eyes flashed black murder. With an economy of motion he went for the older man.

"Jacob, no!" Tom burst out. He dived toward the taller man, yelling for assistance. Two other men from the waiting room helped, and it took all three of them.

The reporter stared at Jacob, aghast, his face going even paler. "Let him loose, boys," he said quietly. "God knows I deserve it. I never should have called her to go in my place."

Jacob shrugged off the other men, but he stood quietly, breathing heavily.

The man hobbled closer. "You must be her brother," he said to Jacob. "I'm Bud Schuman. Kate works with me. I'm so damned sorry—"

"I'm her brother," Tom interrupted, moving forward with a faint smile and a wary glance at Jacob. "And Kate wouldn't blame you, Mr. Schuman. You're a hero of hers. She talks about you all the time."

"I hope she'll talk about me again, even if she cusses a blue streak the whole time," Bud said miserably. "I'm just so sorry. I never think about the risk, you see. I've done this most of my life. And Kate, forgive me, is just one of the boys at the office. We never think of her as a woman. That's why Winthrop gave her the police beat."

Even as he spoke, Morgan Winthrop came storming through the emergency room door. He needed a shave and he looked as if he'd been dragged out of bed.

"Why the hell didn't you call Joey Bradshaw?" Winthrop demanded. "He was sitting home watching reruns of *My Three Sons*, and he carries a piece. At least he could have shot back! So help me God, I ought to slug you, Schuman!"

"Wait your turn," Bud Schuman mused miserably. "There's already a line forming." He indicated a still-smoldering Jacob and a quiet, anguished Tom.

Winthrop glanced at them. "Family, I gather? What can I say?" He jammed his big hands in his raincoat pockets. "Do they know any more now than they did five minutes ago?"

Tom shook his head.

"Sergeant Kovic told me she'd been hit in the abdomen," Winthrop continued gravely.

"Rib cage," Tom countered. "They're taking her into surgery now to see how much damage there is. The bullet passed through a sign, but it came from an automatic Uzi—an illegal weapon with apparently strong velocity. We don't know how bad it is, but the least she's got is a collapsed lung."

Winthrop grimaced. "Poor kid. She's a hell of a reporter, you know. Does features, politics, even the police beat with a flair. Cops like her, too. They'll tell her things that Schuman here can't pry out of them with a fork."

"That's a fact," Bud said. "They like her because she never lies to them. She does exactly what she says she will. Kate never lies."

Jacob turned away, staring blankly at his cigarette. He'd known Kate for eleven years, and strangers knew her better than he did. It was a sobering, painful fact.

"Who is he?" Schuman asked Tom when Jacob was out of earshot. "My God, I thought my number was up before you slowed him down."

"Jacob Cade," Tom replied. "He's a neighbor of ours back home."

"Thought I recognized him," Bud murmured. He smiled sheepishly. "Kate keeps a photo of him in her desk."

"Kate keeps photos of him everywhere." Tom sighed. He stared at the taller man. "I never expected it to hit him this hard. I thought he hated her."

"Hate and love are first cousins," Winthrop said philosophically. He studied the rigid back of the pacing man. "I know how he feels. I've been there." He lifted his shoulders heavily. "How about some coffee? It looks like a long night."

For another hour, Jacob paced while Winthrop and Tom and Bud Schuman sat and reminisced about Kate. And then, all at once, the waiting was over.

They gathered around the surgeon quickly.

"She'll make it," the surgeon told Tom, smiling. "The bullet broke a rib and went through the lower lobe of her lung, where it tore some tissue—we had to remove that lower lobe, but she'll never miss it. We put in a drainage tube to reinflate the lung and drain it and we're giving her blood. Amazing." He shook his head. "Two inches lower and it would have been fatal. Two inches to the outside, and it would have missed her altogether. But she's a pretty fortunate young lady, just the same."

Tom sighed. "Can I see her?"

"She wouldn't know you were there," the surgeon replied. "She'll be in intensive care for tonight, and if she does all right, we'll move her into a private room tomorrow. You can come back in the morning and see her." He clasped the younger man's arm. "Go home and sleep, if you can. I imagine it's been a bad time for you."

"It has. Thanks for all you've done," Tom said with a weary smile. "And I'll go home, but I won't sleep."

The surgeon smiled and walked away.

"Thank God," Bud Schuman sighed. "My God, when they said she'd been hit in the stomach, I thought she was done for. Obviously, she doubled up when the bullet hit..." His mumbled remark was interrupted by an accidental shove from his boss, who saw the horror in Tom's young eyes. Shoptalk wasn't for outsiders. Newsmen got an education in forensic medicine along with a good basic knowledge of clinical details from working with police and coroners.

"Say good-night, Schuman, and let's go. I'll even drive you." Winthrop shook hands with Tom. "I'll keep in touch. Try to get some rest. Call me if I can help."

"Thanks," Tom said.

Winthrop and Schuman left, and Jacob moved to the waiting area, half-empty now, to crush out a cigarette.

"Let's go," Tom said. "I've left the phone number with the desk. They'll call if there's any change."

Jacob turned, his eyes dark and full of pain. "I did that to her," he said numbly.

"Listen, you can't love to order," Tom said with blissful ignorance of what had really happened between Kate and the man standing near him. "Life isn't that simple. Kate will get over you, and she'll be fine. She just needs a little time."

"I hope she has it," Jacob said quietly. "Oh, God, I hope she does."

"I'll make us an omelet," Tom offered as they left the hospital. "Good thing I can cook, or we'd starve by morning."

Back in the apartment, Jacob paced some more. Restlessly, he glanced around the room, learning new things about Kate all the time. He saw what she liked to read, that she did handcrafts, that she loved gardening, that she fed birds outside her window on the small ledge. He learned about the people she'd helped and the affection her neighbors had for her by the bits and pieces of her life scattered around the apartment. And there was no resemblance at all between this woman and the shadowy figure of her he'd built up in his mind.

"Stop worrying, will you?" Tom asked after they'd eaten and he'd watched Jacob push food around on his plate and smoke half a pack of cigarettes, one right after the other. "Nothing is going to change what happened. We need some sleep. I'll take the guest room and you can sleep in Kate's bed."

"No," Jacob said shortly. He turned away, lowering his voice. "No. I'll stay in the guest room."

"All right," Tom said, trying to figure out the older man's odd reaction. "No problem. I'll set the alarm in time to have breakfast before we leave for the hospital."

"Yes." Jacob walked out of the room, grateful that Tom couldn't read the expression in his eyes. Sleep in Kate's bed, with those memories all around... Hell couldn't have been more unwelcome. He hadn't noticed that she'd replaced the bed.

But he didn't sleep. By five o'clock in the morning, he couldn't stand it any longer. He dressed, scribbled a note for Tom and left the apartment.

The nurse in the intensive care unit was a crusty old veteran named Gates, but Jacob got to her. Despite the fact that it wasn't visiting hours, she allowed him ten minutes, without really knowing why. It was something in those dark, tortured eyes. This was a man who wanted absolution, and that young woman he'd come to see wasn't responding as well as Nurse Gates would have liked. Sometimes there was a healing power in a caring voice—the philosophy wasn't based on medical evidence, but it was often true. So she broke a lifelong rule and let him into the small cubicle.

Jacob had only been in a hospital twice—once when his mother had died, and once to visit Kate's grandmother just before she died. But those visits had been nothing like what he was now facing. Kate was hooked to a dozen tubes and wires, and machines made humming, throbbing, whispering noises around her pale, quiet body.

She was stretched out under crisp white sheets in a regulation hospital gown, her hair short now and unwashed, her face pinched and white, her eyes closed, long lashes against pale skin. He looked down at the soft mouth he'd kissed so hungrily, at the body his had possessed, at the slender hands that had clung to him, adored him. He drew in a shuddering breath. Kate.

He drew up the single chair in the cubicle and tossed his gray Stetson onto the floor with careless indifference. He took Kate's free hand—the one that wasn't attached to tubes and wires—in his, and turned it over to look at it. It was cool, and the nails were short, smooth and devoid of color. It was long-fingered, strong for a woman's hand, graceful.

"What a hell of a place for Kate Walker to be," he said, his deep voice quiet and soothing in the mechanical orchestra around him as he spoke to her, just as if she could hear him. "You don't even like mechanical things, do you, Kate? Bird feeders on the window and plants all over the apartment, gardening books on the shelves. No, this isn't your kind of place at all. You need sunlight and open land and room to plant things."

He shifted in the chair, twining her hand slowly into his, studying the way her fingers looked against his, their pale length so natural looking in his firm grasp. "I never knew you at all, did I?" he murmured. "I heard your co-workers talking about you and until then, I don't guess I really thought of you as a person. As a woman, sure. I've wanted you for a long time, Kate. A long, long time. Ever since I saw you kissing Gerald what's-his-name in my swimming pool and found you nude in his arms in the bathhouse, I've been obsessed with you. And once Margo was out of the picture, I figured you were fair game. I could satisfy the hunger I've always felt and you'd stop haunting me."

His face hardened. "But it didn't work out that way. I said some hard things, and you don't even know why I was so cruel that night. It was because I sensed the truth about you. Oh, yes, damn it, I knew deep down that you were innocent, but I was so hungry for you that I wouldn't listen to my conscience. And now it's killing me, Kate."

He cupped her hand in both of his and lifted his eyes to her still figure in the bed. "You see, I didn't know that you loved me," he said, his voice slow and tender and deep with wonder. "My God, nobody ever loved me!" he bit off. "Not like that. There were pictures of me all over the apartment...." He paused, staring blankly at her hand. Somewhere inside, pain was racking him. "Then I knew just how badly I'd hurt you all these years. Accusations, indifference, sarcasm... And you took it all, like a lady. You loved me, and I hurt you in every way there was. That's the hardest thing of all to live with."

His fingers curled hungrily around hers. "Tom doesn't even know why I feel guilty. He doesn't know why you asked for the police beat, but I do. Anything dangerous, isn't that how it goes, Kate? I've tried that route myself these past three weeks. I almost wrecked the car twice, I've ridden murderous stallions, I've started fights. It hasn't been any easier for me than it's been for you. The guilt is killing me. And now this. If you die, how will I go on living? And what if you're carrying my child?" he added quietly, voicing the fear that had driven him here before dawn. "Oh, Kate, I'm...alone. I never minded before. But now..."

He drew her palm to his lips, cherishing it with his mouth, his dark head bent, the hunger in him like a living, breathing thing, and no longer only physical. "Don't die, Kate." His voice broke abruptly, and he paused until he could control it. His fingers tensed and he felt sick and apprehensive. "I don't think I can live in a world that doesn't have you in it somewhere, even if you hate me for the rest of your life."

There was a faint movement in the hand he was holding. He lifted his dark head and looked. Yes. Her fingers had tried to close around his. He stood up slowly, his eyes on her pale, quiet face. She was breathing strongly now, with a steady rhythm. And as he watched, she stirred. Her eyes opened, but they didn't see him. She groaned.

Before he could call Nurse Gates, she was in the room. She patted him on the shoulder. "Good man," she said. "That was just what she needed, to know that someone wanted her to live. Go and have breakfast. She'll be fine now. I've been a nurse for twenty-five years, and believe me, I know a patient on the mend when I see one. This one will go home."

Jacob tried to speak, but he couldn't quite manage the words. He couldn't remember ever being so choked with emotion. Instead, he bent and brushed a kiss against the leathery old cheek and winked.

She smiled up at him, eighteen again for a space of seconds, then turned back to her patient, and Jacob went out of the unit and down the hall to phone Tom.

Kate was out of the intensive care unit by early the next day. But only Tom was allowed in to see her. He didn't have the heart to tell Jacob that Kate had almost had hysterics at just the mention of the older man's name. Letting him into her room had been out of the question.

But at the end of the second day, Jacob asked about it. And Tom took a deep breath and told him the truth.

Jacob hadn't really expected her to remember what he'd said to her in the intensive care unit. In a way, it was a relief, because he'd been vulnerable with her, and that irked him. He'd let his guard down. But never again. So she didn't want him to visit. Well, they'd see.

He sat back down in the waiting room, picking up a copy of *Field and Stream* to thumb through.

"Jacob, you did understand what I said?" Tom asked hesitantly.

"I understood. But she'll see me sooner or later, if I have to sit here until hell freezes over." He smiled vaguely in Tom's direction and kept reading.

"Why do you want to?"

Jacob didn't look up. "I don't know."

"Terrific answer," Tom mumbled as he walked away.

Jacob looked after him with dark, troubled eyes. How could he have confided to Tom that he had to know if Kate was pregnant? With a heavy sigh, he stared blankly down at the magazine. And maybe it was more than that. He wanted to see her moving, see her eyes open, even if they were filled with hatred. He wanted to see for himself that she was all right before he left town. He'd have to go back soon. Work was piling up. But right now, Kate was what mattered the most.

When Tom went back into the room, she was propped up in bed, still a little drowsy from the medication, favoring the left side of her rib cage, which was bandaged. They'd made a small incision about six-inches long beside the bullet hole for the exploratory surgery. It was held together by staples, of all things, and it was sore, like her broken rib. There hadn't been anything they could do about her rib, but they would put her in a rib belt when the drainage tube came out in three or four days, and that would hold it in place until it healed.

"He won't go home," Tom said from the doorway, smiling. "He says he'll sit there until hell freezes over or until you decide to talk to him, whichever comes first."

Kate stared at her hands on the sheet, trying to ignore the wild beating of her heart. Jacob's stubbornness was unexpected. But why should he want to see her? She thought of the hundred-dollar bill and was surprised at how much the memory hurt, despite all that had happened in the meantime.

"He may have a long wait," she said drowsily. "I don't want to talk to him."

Tom took the chair beside her bed and sat down. She did look like hell, he thought. She was pale and drawn, and her dark hair had no luster at all. Her lips were faintly cracked with dryness and her eyes were deep-shadowed with pain and fatigue. But, then, Jacob didn't look much better himself. He frowned.

"Kate, what's going on?" he asked gently.

Her thin eyebrows shot up. "What do you mean?"

"Something happened between you and Jacob. He's been like a wild man since you got shot. Bud Schuman came into the waiting room and it took three of us to keep Jacob from killing him."

Surprise after surprise, she thought numbly. She stared at her brother with wide, curious eyes. "Jacob did?"

"He sat with you in the intensive care unit, too," he added quietly. "I don't know what he said, but apparently they think whatever it was helped get you back on the right track."

She shifted, grimacing. "I don't remember."

"I guess not. You were pretty much out of it about then. Thank God for modern medicine and the sign that slowed the bullet down a little before it hit you."

"It wasn't Bud's fault," she said.

"You're the only person with that particular point of view," he assured her. "Winthrop threatened to fire him, and he wasn't too pleased with himself, either."

"Did someone get the story?"

"You were the story," he replied. "Front page and a banner headline."

"I told you I'd get the front page one day," she smiled wanly.

"What a heck of a way to go about it," he said with a grin. He leaned forward, holding her hand. "Jacob hurt you somehow, is that it?"

She forced herself to meet his eyes and smile. "We had a horrible argument," she said, then added, "which I don't want to discuss."

"Oh." He shrugged. "Well, you don't have to worry about having him make sarcastic remarks about your morals anymore, at least. I set him straight. I told him everything."

She went two shades paler and her heart stopped beating. "What did he say?" she asked in a whisper.

"He didn't say anything, actually." He studied her face. "He went as white as you just did and the one glimpse I got of his eyes was enough." He paused for a minute. "Yes, I know, Kate, we agreed that we'd never tell anyone. But Jacob isn't anyone. And you love him."

Her eyes widened, darkened. "Oh, Tom, you didn't tell him that, did you?" she asked, and her whole expression was pleading.

She'd been through enough already, he thought, and Jacob wouldn't mention it. Why make it worse? "Would I tell him something like that?" he said, evading the question.

"I hope you wouldn't," she replied. "I don't have a lot of pride left."

"He'll sit there for a week if he has to, you know," Tom said after a minute.

She stared at him without speaking. He didn't know why Jacob wanted to see her, but she did. And because she did, she gave in, fighting the nervousness and apprehension she felt at having to see Jacob again.

"All right," she said. "Let him come in. But only for five minutes."

He smiled. "Be right back."

Kate sat and watched the door, her eyes unnaturally wide, her face even whiter and more strained than it had been. And minutes later, the door opened slowly and she bit her lip to keep from crying. Jacob had hurt her terribly, and not just physically. Over and over again, she'd heard his bitter words, felt the cold rustle of that hundred-dollar bill he'd put in the towel against her breasts. It was all she could do not to break down at just the sight of him.

Six

It was impossible to look into those dark eyes. After one quick glance at his rigid features, she averted her gaze to his boots. Gray boots, highly polished, crafted with expensive hand-tooled leather, they matched the hat dangling idly from his lean hand. A Stetson, too; she recognized the distinct JBS-initialed silver pin and feather hatband decoration of the true Stetson. Jacob never wore any other kind of hat.

"How are you?" he asked as he approached the bed.

Her heart pounded wildly, her breath caught in her dry throat. "They say I'll be fine in about six weeks or so."

"That isn't what I asked."

He was much too close. She could smell the particularly spicy brand of after-shave he wore, and a faint leathery scent on top of it. He was wearing a dark blue suit, and she hated noticing how it flattered his dark complexion.

"I hurt," she said curtly.

"Yes, I know, Kate."

Surely that note in his voice wasn't tenderness. But she had to look and see, and the minute she lifted her eyes, his dark ones trapped them.

"You're still pale, but at least you're conscious this time," he murmured.

"What do you want, Jacob?" she asked tersely.

"To see for myself that you're healing properly." His dark eyes dropped to the sheet her slender hands were clutching. "You came close to the edge."

"I'll be all right. You can stop feeling guilty. I'm tough."

He smiled faintly. "You've had to be, haven't you?" he asked, and his eyes held new knowledge of her.

"Tom shouldn't have told you," she returned. She felt shaky inside, having him know about the past. "I've never even talked to Margo about it."

"You do realize that if I'd known, I'd never have made any snap judgments about you, despite the circumstances?" he asked gently.

"You enjoy thinking the worst of me."

He shrugged. "I guess it seemed that way to you." He twirled the hat in his fingers and stared at her for a long moment.

"I'm not pregnant," she told him bluntly, flushing a little as she guessed correctly the question he was about to ask. "That should make you very happy."

He pulled up the chair beside the bed and sat down in it slowly. He crossed his legs and rested the hat on one knee. His hand automatically reached for a cigarette and just as quickly withdrew without it. Her lung hadn't completely inflated. The tube, which was still draining fluid out of the lung they'd operated on, wouldn't come

out until the X rays showed that the lung was fully inflated again, or so the surgeon had told him and Tom.

"Babies shouldn't be made that way," he said finally,
leaning back to watch her reaction. "Not out of a man's
blind passion and selfish motives. I know you hate my
guts, Kate, and I don't blame you. The way I treated you
that night was unforgivable. If it helps, I'll never get over
handing you that hundred-dollar bill. I haven't slept an
entire night since."

She lowered her eyes to the high polish of his boots and
felt her body tremble with reaction as the memory came
washing over her. Jacob, touching her, kissing her, his
body rigid with passion...

"I don't want to remember," she whispered fiercely.

He knew why, too, and just barely escaped a heated
reply. But God knew, she was entitled to a little retribu-
tion. He'd hurt her terribly that night. He dropped his hat
on the floor and leaned forward. "Come home with me,
Kathryn."

Her body stiffened convulsively under the sheet.
"What?"

"You can't stay by yourself in Chicago. Tom's got to
go back to work in a few days. You won't have anybody
to take care of you."

"I can take care of myself," she said tightly. "Thank
you just the same."

He got up, towering over her, his eyes deeply troubled
as he reached down and took her hand in his, refusing to
let go even when she tried to withdraw it.

"Don't fight me," he said tautly. "I'm all too aware
that I helped put you here. At least let me try to make up
for it in the only way I can."

Her face felt hot. She stared at his white shirt, hating her own embarrassment and shame. Her eyes closed. "Go away, Jacob."

"A bullet might be kinder than sending me away."

She frowned and opened her eyes to stare up at him. He didn't look as if he were kidding. His face showed nothing of what he felt, but his eyes were haunted.

"I have to do something, Kate," he said quietly. "I know you hate me, but—"

"Oh, no," she said. Her eyes ran over his dark face like hands. "No, it isn't . . . hatred." She lowered her gaze to the strong hand holding hers. "It isn't even completely your fault. I could have stopped you if I'd told you the truth. I knew that. But there had been too many years of antagonism. I was too embarrassed to talk to you about my hang-ups, and afterward. . ." The color blazed in her face. "I wanted to die," she whispered, and the tears stung her eyes suddenly. "I'm so ashamed."

"Kate." There was an anguished tone in his voice. He brought her hand to his mouth and kissed the palm hotly, hungrily. "Honey, don't. Please don't."

She turned her face into the pillow and the tears flooded down her cheeks. He bent over her, his free hand gently smoothing her hair, his lips touching her forehead, her eyebrows, her closed eyes. She smelled him, could almost taste him. No, she thought, he felt only pity and guilt for her, and she didn't want those emotions from him.

"No," she pleaded. Her eyes opened, wide and dark green, frightened eyes that had a hunted look. "Jacob, I don't want—"

He put a long finger across her pale lips. His eyes searched hers much too intensely. "Kate, I've never tried to be gentle," he said hesitantly, as if he were finding the words with difficulty. "I'm not even sure I know how. Don't push me away before I get started."

"I don't want pity," she whispered tearfully.

"Neither do I," he whispered back. He traced her lips with his finger, fascinated by the way they pursed at the light movement. "Do you like that?" he asked absently.

She had to hold onto her pride. She had to remember how horrible he'd been to her. His finger tracing her lips was making it difficult to think.

"Yes, you do like it, don't you?" he breathed. He bent his dark head and watched her eyes close helplessly as his lips brushed with aching tenderness over hers. His nose brushed against her cheek as he nuzzled her face with his.

"Jacob," she protested, but it was more moan than objection.

He brought her hand to his hard cheek and pressed it there, palm down, savoring its soft coolness. "I want my hundred-dollar bill back."

It was the last thing, the very last thing, she'd expected him to say. Her eyes flew open, astonished.

"You heard me." He nibbled her thumb sensually, his dark eyes watching her. "And I take back every damned insulting remark I've ever made. Would you like to know why I insulted you like that with money, Kate?"

"I . . . because I ran from you, I guess," she faltered.

He shook his head. "You hurt my pride," he said quietly. "I didn't want to believe you were innocent. I hurt you, but I didn't realize it. I was convinced that you were experienced and that I hadn't measured up to your other men."

Her lips parted helplessly. "I . . . didn't realize," she whispered. "Did you, really?"

Incredible, the way it felt to talk to her like this. His blood felt as if it contained bubbles. He'd never admitted such a thing before. But honesty with Kate was easier than he'd expected. She didn't snap or use sarcasm or make wild accusations.

He actually smiled, and his smile was genuine. "I did, really."

Her eyes fell to his chest. She wanted to explain to him why she'd said what she did, what she'd been feeling. But she was painfully shy with him now, and the memory alone was enough to embarrass her.

He brushed her hair away from her forehead. "Do you know, I've never come closer to an apology in my life."

She smiled faintly. "I never expected one."

"I'm a hard case, Kate. I'll break before I bend an inch. That's the truth. I can't change."

As his lips touched her forehead, she felt a sense of amazement. This couldn't be Jacob. Perhaps she was dreaming. Or in a coma. Or dead.

Her eyes lifted to his, soft with tenderness, and he caught his breath. Yes, she loved him, all right. Apparently love endured anything, if that aching sweetness in her eyes was anything to go by. With his fingers, he touched her mouth, fascinated by it, by that radiance that chased away all the shadows, all the pain. She loved him.

He frowned, because he still wasn't sure that he wanted to be loved. But she was different from his usual kind of woman; a new experience. He'd grown jaded, cynical about women. They only wanted his money or a good time. But here was Kate, whom he'd known half her life, and suddenly sex was something profound and he didn't want anyone else.

"You look stunned," she remarked curiously. "Are you all right?"

He shifted, standing up straight, although his hand retained possession of hers. "I don't know."

The more
you love romance . . .
the more
you'll love this offer

FREE!

Mail this heart today! (See inside)

**Join us on a Silhouette® Honeymoon
and we'll give you
4 free books
A free manicure set
And a free mystery gift**

IT'S A
SILHOUETTE HONEYMOON —
A SWEETHEART
OF A FREE OFFER!

HERE'S WHAT YOU GET:

1. Four New Silhouette Desire® Novels — FREE!

Take a Silhouette Honeymoon with your four exciting romances
— yours FREE from Silhouette Books. Each of these hot-off-the-
press novels brings you the passion and tenderness of today's
greatest love stories . . . your free passports to bright new worlds
of love and foreign adventure.

2. A compact manicure set — FREE!

You'll love your beautiful manicure set — an elegant and useful accessory to carry in your hand-
bag. Its rich burgundy case is a perfect
expression of your style and good taste — and
it's yours free with this offer!

3. An Exciting Mystery Bonus — FREE!

You'll be thrilled with this surprise gift. It will be the source of
many compliments, as well as a useful and attractive addition to
your home.

4. Money-Saving Home Delivery!

Join the Silhouette Desire subscriber service and enjoy the convenience of previewing 6 new books every month delivered right
to your home. Each book is yours for only $2.24 — 26¢ less per
book than what you pay in stores. And there is no extra charge for
postage and handling. Great savings plus total convenience add
up to a sweetheart of a deal for you!

5. Free Newsletter!

You'll get our monthly newsletter, packed with news on your
favorite writers, upcoming books, even recipes from your favorite authors.

6. More Surprise Gifts!

Because our home subscribers are our most valued readers, we'll
be sending you additional free gifts from time to time — as a token
of our appreciation.

**START YOUR SILHOUETTE HONEYMOON TODAY — JUST
COMPLETE, DETACH AND MAIL YOUR FREE-OFFER CARD**

Get your fabulous gifts
ABSOLUTELY FREE!

MAIL THIS CARD TODAY.

PLACE
HEART STICKER
HERE

GIVE YOUR HEART TO SILHOUETTE

Yes! Please send me my four Silhouette Desire novels FREE, along with my free manicure set and free mystery gift as explained on the opposite page.

NAME _____
(PLEASE PRINT)

ADDRESS _____ APT. _____

CITY _____ STATE _____

ZIP CODE _____

225 CIY JAYA

Prices subject to change. Offer limited to one per household and not valid to present subscribers.

SILHOUETTE BOOKS "NO-RISK" GUARANTEE

— There's no obligation to buy — and the free books and gifts remain yours to keep.

— You pay the lowest price possible and receive books before they appear in stores.

— You may end your subscription any time — just write and let us know.

START YOUR
SILHOUETTE HONEYMOON TODAY.
JUST COMPLETE, DETACH AND MAIL YOUR
FREE-OFFER CARD.

If offer card below is missing, write to:
Silhouette Books, 901 Fuhrmann Blvd., P.O. Box 9013, Buffalo, N.Y. 14240-9013

"What is it?"

He scowled down at her, searching her face, her eyes. He'd been less wary while she was unconscious, when he was faced with the possibility of losing her forever. Now, with the obstacles out of the way, the old fears were back. Kate wasn't the kind of woman a man played around with. If he started anything with her now, he'd have to finish it. That meant marriage and kids—responsibilities he'd always thought of in the distant future, not the present. Kate loved him. But did he want that?

She didn't understand the sudden shift in his attitude. He'd gone away without moving a muscle. And then it dawned on her: He was afraid she'd die and he'd have her on his conscience. Now he was feeling relief and guilt and a little shame, and he was already regretting his impulsive offer. Jacob didn't want anything permanent; he'd made that clear the night he seduced her.

She felt an overwhelming sadness. He didn't want anything from her except to be forgiven for what he'd said and done. That was all. She might love him, but he had nothing to give her. She stared up at him quietly. Well, at least he didn't know how she felt. That was the only consolation she had. And she wouldn't let him know, either.

"It's all right," she said unexpectedly, and forced a smile. "You don't have to worry about me anymore. I'll be fine. I think I'll go to New York with Tom. I can stay in his apartment while I'm getting back on my feet."

She said it too quickly. He saw immediately what she was trying to do. It hurt him that she cared enough to put his comfort above her own, even when she needed him so desperately. She didn't want to go to New York, but she didn't feel welcome at Warlance.

"You're reading me wrong, Kate," he said quietly. "I'm not thinking of ways to back out of the invitation."

She flushed. "You seemed uncomfortable about it," she replied.

"I'm uncomfortable about a lot of things lately." He looked and sounded tired. Dead tired. There were dark circles under his eyes and he looked as worn as he felt. All that waiting. Tom hadn't been alone; Jacob had been with him every step of the way.

"You need sleep," she said abruptly.

"Do I?" He stuck his hands in his pockets and stood beside the bed, looking down at her pale, quiet face. "You need it more."

"I don't sleep well," she confessed. "I keep hearing the bullets."

"All the more reason to get out of the city for a while. You can't work for several weeks. You'd probably go crazy in your apartment." He pursed his lips. "Come with me. I'll build you a greenhouse."

Her face went two shades of pink and she stared at him wildly. "What?" she breathed, overcome that he should hit accidentally on the one big dream of her life lately.

"You garden, don't you?" he mused. "You have dozens of books on horticulture. I'll make sure you have a place to practice your hobby while you're recuperating."

It was like a dream coming true. She wanted to be with him, even though she knew it was only guilt that motivated him. To be near him, just to be allowed to sit and look at him, was all of heaven. That, and a greenhouse, too. She had to be dreaming.

"That would be a lot of trouble," she began, trying to be sensible.

"Not particularly," he replied. "I've got the space, and there are a few experiments I'd like to try with new strains of forage grasses."

"Well..."

"You're running out of excuses," he observed.

She sighed, folding her hands. "I'd like to go," she confessed. "But I'll just be in the way, and Janet has enough to do. And Barbara won't like it," she added, avoiding his eyes.

He hadn't seen Barbara Dugan in so long that she was little more than a memory. He blinked. "What does Barbara have to do with it?" he asked curiously.

"Everybody says you'll marry her eventually. Her land adjoins Warlance."

"My God, Kate, so does Billy Kramer's, but I'll be damned if I'd want to marry him for it."

His dry sense of humor was something she'd forgotten during the long antagonism of the years. She was the one person he'd never joked with in recent memory.

"I just don't want to foul up your life," she said doggedly, ignoring the humor.

"As if it isn't pretty fouled up now," he murmured, watching her closely. "You won't cramp my style, Kate, or get in my way. I'll take care of you until you can take care of yourself again."

She was weakening. Her big, soft eyes searched his, vulnerable and frightened.

He moved closer to the bed, his protective instincts aroused and bubbling over. "I won't hurt you again," he said quietly. "I swear to God I won't."

Her eyes fell. "All right," she sighed. "I'll go with you, if you're sure—"

"I'm sure."

She lay back again and closed her eyes with a weary sigh, wincing as the movement caused her pain. "Shot's worn off." She grimaced.

"I'll tell the desk on my way out," he replied. "I've got a few details to take care of." He brushed his hand lightly over her hair. "Can I bring you anything?"

"No, thank you," she said.

"Then I'll see you later."

He paused at the door to look back. She was in pain again, and in a good deal of it from her rigid posture. He went past Tom, motioning the younger man to follow, and explained at the desk what was wrong. The nurse smiled and immediately went to take care of Kate.

"What did she say?" Tom asked him.

"I talked her into going home with me," Jacob said. "She'll do better in the country, and you can't watch her and work at the same time."

"I'm not arguing," Tom mused. "I'm just wondering how you managed to convince her. She said the two of you had had a royal falling out."

"We did. But maybe we understand each other a little better than we did."

Tom lifted his eyebrows. "You didn't tell her what I told you?"

Jacob shook his head. "I didn't think revelations would be good for her state of mind. And you'd better believe I won't take advantage of how she feels while she's with me."

"I never thought you would," Tom said honestly. "You aren't the type to play around with virgins."

It was a good thing that Tom didn't know the whole truth, Jacob thought with bitter humor. "I want to go and speak to her boss about a leave of absence. She'll be upset if her job's gone when she comes back."

So much for Tom's hope that Jacob might be feeling something deeper for Kate. As he feared, the other man felt only guilt and pity. Jacob was already making plans for her return to Chicago. How Kate would hate knowing that. Tom smiled forcibly. "That might be a good idea."

"I'll be back afterwhile."

Jacob turned and left Tom in the waiting room. He didn't know why, but he needed to get away, to think.

He walked for over an hour, his mind blank, seeing the city without really noticing anything about it. He turned finally and went down the block where the newspaper office that Kate worked for was located.

Morgan Winthrop was sitting at his massive desk, giving somebody hell over the telephone when Jacob walked in. As soon as Winthrop saw the other man, he cut the conversation short and hung up.

"How's Kate?" he said without conventional greetings.

"She's sitting up today, for short stretches, at least," Jacob told him. "I'm taking her home with me to recuperate. I want to pay her salary while she's out and let her think the paper's doing it."

"And I thought I was a blunt man," Winthrop mused.

"It saves time to come to the point." He studied the older man. "She's too proud to let me pay her bills, so it's the last resort."

"Okay. I'll set it up with the payroll department and we'll settle it between ourselves." He named a figure that Kate drew each week.

"Hell," Jacob muttered, "I spend more than that on fertilizer and salt blocks!"

"People don't work at reporting to get rich."

"So I see. All right, I'll send a check over in the morning. And not a word to Kate."

Morgan Winthrop was darker and broader than Jacob, and his eyes had a faintly haunted look. "Maybe I'm talking out of turn, but do you know how Kate feels about you?"

Jacob's face hardened. He almost didn't answer at all. "Yes," he said finally. "But she doesn't know that I do."

"My wife and I had a major misunderstanding two years ago," Morgan Winthrop said quietly. "She went away to Paris to recover from the argument we had and I let her. The day she was due to leave for home, the taxicab that was taking her to the airport was involved in a wreck and she was killed instantly. Don't ever assume that you have all the time in the world to clear things up."

"Yes. I learned that three nights ago," Jacob said. "How did you know?"

"Kate keeps a photo of you in her desk."

Jacob's eyes narrowed as he studied the older man. After a minute, he slowly pulled out his wallet, opened a section of it with plastic inserts and showed something to Winthrop.

The older man only nodded. "Take care of her."

"I always did," Jacob replied. He put up the wallet. "Not a word about the paycheck."

Morgan Winthrop smiled. "What paycheck?"

Bud Schuman was at his desk when Jacob started out. He deliberately dropped a pencil and bent over to find it.

Jacob didn't even glance in his direction. But when he got out the door, he was chuckling softly to himself. The old reporter was a character, and if Jacob had been just a little more forgiving, he might have spoken to him. But he couldn't forget that Schuman might have cost Kate her life with that tip.

He stopped by Kate's apartment long enough to have dinner, and then he went back to the hospital. He found a stranger sitting by Kate's bed holding her hand.

It took all his willpower not to lift the man by the collar and drop him out the window.

"Well, well, you must be Kate's brother. I've heard a lot about you," the tall, heavyset blond man said pleasantly, rising to shake hands. "I'm Roger Dean. I work for a nearby weekly newspaper, and I've been trying to seduce Kate for years without success."

Kate turned beet red and wished she felt well enough to get under the bed. Jacob had turned an odd shade of dusky red and his black eyes were flashing danger signals.

"That isn't Tom," Kate said quickly. "Roger, this is Jacob Cade. His niece and I are best friends."

"Sorry about the mistake. Nice to meet you, anyway," Roger grinned pleasantly. "Just like Kate to jump in front of a bullet. I've warned her for years about following the police around...."

"Kate's coming home with me to South Dakota," Jacob said, his voice pleasant enough. But his stance was threatening, and his eyes were saying a lot more. He looked purely possessive—dangerously possessive as he moved to Kate's side and deliberately blocked Roger's attempt to take her hand.

Roger wasn't thick. He knew immediately what was going on. He smiled at Kate.

"Glad to see you're better, kid. Now don't go roping steers and such, okay? And I'll see you again before you leave."

"All right," Kate said softly. "Thanks for coming, Roger."

"I wouldn't have missed it. I always wanted to be part of a gun battle. Oh, well, maybe I'll get caught in a tornado or something one day. See you, pretty girl. Nice to have met you, Mr. . . . Cade? So long."

Jacob watched him go with an expression Kate couldn't quite classify. He frightened her a little.

"Damned prissy lunatic," he muttered under his breath. "Is he unbalanced?"

"He was only kidding, Jacob. I went out with him once or twice."

He turned on his heel, his gaze possessive. "Never again," he said, without apology for the command in his tone.

She stopped breathing. At least it felt like that. Her green eyes searched his dark ones with wary curiosity. "You don't own me, Jacob," she began hesitantly.

"Under the circumstances, I have every right in the world to feel possessive about you," he replied. "I don't want another man's hands on you, ever."

She flushed crimson.

"Yes, I know," he continued, unabashed, "you don't want mine on you, either. I don't blame you. But one day, I may even change your mind about that. Now, let me tell you what I've arranged with Winthrop about your leave of absence."

He sat down and told her the fiction without jeopardizing the fact, and she was too bemused by his attitude toward Roger to question any of it. By the time her mind was clear, Tom was there and the conversation became general. The men were still talking when she finally slept, just as visiting hours ended.

Seven

To get them back to South Dakota, Jacob had wanted to charter a private plane, a large twin-engine one with plenty of room for Kate to relax in without being cramped or crowded. But the doctor had said that because of her lung injury, she wouldn't be able to fly for at least two months.

"But you hate flying," she blurted out when he mentioned it in the hospital.

He shrugged. "I could have managed. But the doctor said you couldn't fly."

"It's only a rib...."

"And part of your lung," he continued for her, his gaze sharp and challenging. "So I've chartered a bus. A big one. Dad is going to pick us up in Pierre with the Lincoln and I'll send someone to Chicago to pick up the Mercedes."

"You're going to a lot of trouble."

He lifted his chin, studying her downcast face. "A little pampering isn't going to hurt you."

"Getting used to it from you is ironic, though," she said.

He hesitated uncharacteristically and studied his clasped hands. "Old enemies, is that how it goes? But we weren't always, Kate," he reminded her. "There was a time when we were friends."

She smiled, remembering. "You were kind to me, then."

"You were the only friend Margo had," he said. "You still are. It's made things rough, in more ways than you realize."

"Yes. You didn't feel free to seduce me as long as she was around. You had to set a good example for her, didn't you?" The minute the words were out, she regretted them.

"You make it sound cold-blooded," he said with surprising patience. He sounded almost kind, and when she looked up, his eyes were indulgent. "Kate, I wanted you. But even then, if you'd said no, I'd have backed off. You see, I hadn't counted on just how little self-control I was going to have when things heated up. I lost my head when I began to kiss you in the car."

She hadn't thought Jacob ever lost control, although she remembered how rapidly he'd lost it that night. She'd pushed him beyond his limits. Perhaps he was still angry about it. She remembered the way they'd kissed, too, and the aching sweetness of his mouth on hers. It seemed like such a long time ago.

"I suppose that happens from time to time," she said noncommittally.

"It doesn't happen to me."

She looked up into half-amused, half-irritated dark eyes. "Oh."

His brows drew down just a little as he studied her. "Didn't anyone ever tell you that men get unmanageable pretty fast when a woman responds without restraint."

Her eyes searched his, frankly fascinated with the tenderness in them. "No. I read a lot of books, though...."

"Someday you and I are going to have to have a little talk about birds and bees," he murmured dryly.

"That really won't be necessary. I don't have any inclination to build nests or make honey."

He nodded. "That's understandable. But eventually you're going to learn that women get as much pleasure from sex as men do."

"They do not!" she shot back, remembering the hollow, incomplete feeling, the anguished frustration she'd felt that night.

"Not the first time, certainly," he said easily. "Not when the man takes it all and gives nothing back. That's another first, in case you're interested. I'm not a selfish man."

This conversation was getting out of hand. It was too soon for such an intimate talk with him. She toyed with the sheet. "When are they going to let me out of here? Has Tom checked?"

He pursed his lips. "Evasive maneuvers, I see," he mused. "All right, I'll let you get away with it this time. Your doctor says you can go next Friday morning, if you're still doing this well by then. That will make it about the tenth day and, according to your doctor, that's considered a pretty short stay for this kind of injury."

"I'm so tired of bed," she said with a sigh.

"Don't expect to climb trees the minute you're discharged," he countered. "You won't be exercising very much until that broken rib heals and that will take about five more weeks."

"What medical school did you graduate from?" she murmured with a faint smile.

"I got in a fight once and had two ribs caved in with a two-by-four," he said. "I remember how it hurt to even dance with girls, much less do anything more strenuous."

There were so many questions she wanted to ask, but it wouldn't do to put them into words. He wouldn't like it. He felt sorry for her, guilty for seducing her. That was all he felt—he wanted no part of her emotional hunger. She had to keep that in mind before she made a fool of herself.

"No comment?" he asked.

She shrugged, grimacing. "I don't have any right to be curious about your private life, Jacob," she said quietly.

"No right or no interest?" he asked, his voice deep and soft.

Her eyes found the floor and stayed there, hiding from him. "Wouldn't you like some coffee?"

"I guess so," he sighed. He got to his feet, gazing at her intently. "Can I bring you anything?"

She shook her head. What she wanted, nobody could bring her.

Unexpectedly, he reached down and touched her hair gently, feeling a sudden protective stirring deep inside himself. "I know it's a lot to ask, but will you try to stop looking back? There's nothing either of us can do to change what happened."

"I know that," she said, her voice subdued. "I don't blame you, Jacob."

"Don't you?" He sounded bitter, and when she looked at him, his expression was hard and mocking.

"My father was...was a fanatic," she said softly. "You can't imagine what it was like."

"Oh, but I can," he said. His dark eyes searched hers. "If I'd had any inkling of your upbringing, I'd never have touched you."

"Don't you think I knew that?" she asked, vulnerability in her tone as she watched him.

His hand smoothed the dull sheen of her short hair. "Did you want me so badly, little one?" he asked tenderly.

Her lower lip trembled and tears threatened. "I wanted..." She bit her lip, hard. Love, she could have added. Just a little love, a little respite from the loneliness and longing of years. She closed her eyes. "It doesn't matter now. I'm very tired."

She was closing up like a flower at night, shutting him out. He could imagine what she was about to admit, but she didn't want him to know how she really felt. His lean fingers brushed her pale cheek.

"Get some sleep. I'll come back when Tom does."

"He was going to pack some things for me."

"He already has. Your case is sitting beside your front door."

Her eyes opened, the expression in them was very vulnerable. "Jacob, I could still go with him...."

"He can't look after you and work. I can."

"You shouldn't have to. I'm not your responsibility."

He almost smiled at her dogged expression. "Kate," he said softly, "hasn't it occurred to you yet that I might want you to be?"

"No, it hasn't, and no, you don't," she returned. "You feel guilty and sorry for me. You needn't pretend it's anything else, and I don't want to go home with you on sufferance—oh!''

Before she could finish the tirade, his mouth had moved softly over hers, touching her lips with aching tenderness. She smelled his spicy after-shave, tasted the faint tobacco tartness of his breath. It was all she could do to keep from responding.

"I don't have time for guilt and pity," he whispered against her moist lips. "I'm a busy man with autumn coming on. But I'll make sure you have enough on your mind to keep you from brooding while you heal. Now stop hunting for excuses and go to sleep. We've got a long trip ahead of us."

Her fingers curled beside her head with impotent anguish. He was sorry for her; she knew he was. He'd regret this generous impulse, and he had no idea what his remorse would do to her. His kindness was a double-edged sword, taunting her with the shadow of an emotion he'd never feel for her.

His hand smoothed over her fist, his own fingers untangling hers in a slow, sensuous caress while he held her wide eyes.

"I know you don't trust me," he murmured. "Your emotions are like these fingers, Kathryn, tied in knots to protect them from me. There's no need for that anymore, but I'm going to have to prove it to you. So just take your time, honey, and we'll go from here. No more looking behind us." He eased her fist open and brought the palm to his warm mouth. "Sleep tight."

She watched him go with troubled eyes. Life was getting more complicated by the minute.

Tom went with them to the ranch, just to see Kate settled, and she thought secretly that Jacob was glad of the company. He was impatient. He didn't like riding any more than he liked flying, and it was an all-day trip from Chicago to Pierre with infrequent stops to eat and rest. Jacob passed the time by talking to Tom while Kate curled up in a long row of seats she had all to herself, with the armrests lifted out of the way.

She'd insisted on getting into the bus on her own, but she was sore and weak by the time they reached the bus station in sprawling Pierre. Jacob lifted her easily, tenderly, and carried her to his waiting Lincoln, with his father behind the wheel.

"Hi, Kate," Hank Cade grinned, his silvery hair blowing in the breeze. "Hello, Tom. How was the trip, son?" he asked Jacob.

"Just great," Jacob said through his teeth as he eased Kate into the back seat so that she could stretch out.

"He hates planes," Hank told Tom who was climbing in beside Kate. "But he hates riding in buses just as much."

"Most sane people hate flying," Jacob replied. He opened the driver's door. "Move over," he told his father.

Hank glared at him indignantly. "I can drive," he retorted.

"Then do it, but not in my car," Jacob replied. "I'm not stupid enough to ride with you."

"I'm a better driver than you are! At least I never wrecked more than one car!"

"Those accidents weren't my fault," Jacob said imperturbably, sliding into the car with enough force to move his father to one side. "I was hit all three times."

"Because you pulled out in front of people, tailgated and ran stop signs!" Hank accused.

"I'm a good driver," Jacob muttered. He started the car and shot off away from the airport, narrowly missing a car that had just turned into the parking lot. "Damned fool," he muttered at the stunned, innocent driver. "Should have watched where he was going."

Kate was trying not to laugh. She looked at Tom and almost burst with suppressed amusement.

"He was a damned fool, all right," Hank agreed, "for getting onto a highway when you were driving a car!"

"Calm down," Jacob mused. "Remember your blood pressure."

"Why should I when it doesn't ever remember me."

"Why didn't Janet drive you out here?"

"Our housekeeper knew she'd have to ride back with you, so she very sensibly stayed behind to fix lunch," Hank replied.

Jacob glared at him. "I drive better than you do."

"So could I, if I could see!"

"Have your damned cataracts taken care of."

"No fancy doctor's cutting on my eyes!"

Kate exchanged an amused glance with Tom. These fights between father and son were familiar territory. The exchange brought back gentle memories of another time, when Jacob had been an easygoing, caring friend instead of the sarcastic stranger of more recent years. The passengers in the back seat kept quiet and listened all the way to Warlance, while Jacob and Hank went back and forth about everything from the state of local politics to the condition of the cattle on the ranch.

Minutes later, they wound up the long dirt road that led to Warlance. Like most of this part of South Dakota, the country was rolling plains with trees in only occasional patterns around the far-flung houses. The state was sixteenth in the nation in land area, but forty-fifth in population. It had what Jacob had always called "elbow room," and in a big way. Warlance's nearest neighbor, the Dugan ranch, was over ten miles away.

The big white two-story house that Hank Cade's grandfather had built was set in a frame of oak trees, while cattle grazed in the moderate warmth of a northwestern fall along tributaries of the Missouri River, which divided South Dakota right down the middle. To the northeast was Pierre, the state capital. To the southwest were the Badlands. To the far west were the Black Hills. To the north was the Cheyenne River Indian Reservation. All around, there was history. To Kate, the wide-open country with its smooth hills and isolated buttes was a treat to the eye. Chicago had given her a bad case of claustrophobia at first— She was used to clear horizons and a satisfying lack of trees to clutter up the view. And nothing in the city, despite its beauty, had made up for the lack of open land and sunshine and air as fresh as the winter snow.

"I'd forgotten how large Warlance was," Tom remarked as they wound up the drive. Big Hereford bulls grazed on one side of the dirt road, heifers and calves on the other.

"It seems to get bigger all the time when Jay isn't around," Hank had the grace to admit. He grimaced. "It's one crisis after another. And I've been saving the worst until last, son. Chuck Gray quit yesterday."

Jacob glared at his father. "Why?"

"He said to tell you he'd rounded up one damned bull too many," he replied. "You might remember that fall is the season we round up the bulls," he told those in the back seat. "Somebody always gets stepped on or gored or kicked. This year it was Chuck. He went to work for a ranch over in Montana."

"Damn it," Jacob cursed as he pulled up at the steps. "He was the best wrangler I ever had."

"You should have let him wrangle horses instead of telling him to help round up bulls, then, son, like I told you," Hank said smugly. "If you'd have listened to me—"

"I did listen to you, damn it. You're the geezer who told me to let him help round up bulls!"

Hank shrugged. "Well, then, why did you listen to me?"

Jacob snapped off the engine with a vicious switch of his fingers and glared at his father. "Why in hell don't you go off sailing to Tahiti like you always swear you're going to?"

"Now, son, if I did that, who'd look out for you?"

Kate started to laugh. "I'm sorry," she apologized, trying to stifle her mouth when Jacob glared toward her. "I was just thinking about . . . something."

"Sure. I'll bet." Jacob got out of the car and lifted her out, ignoring her protests, as Tom and Hank paused to get the luggage from the trunk.

"Janet! Open the front door!" Jacob called, his voice carrying all the way to the corral, where two cowboys looked their way.

"You could break glasses with that voice!" the old, heavyset woman in a green housedress and pink bedroom slippers grumbled as she ambled out the door and held it open. "Afternoon, Kate. It's good to see you. I'm not making any comments about him, though. I was just getting used to peace and quiet, and here he comes back. I bet he's gotten Mr. Hank in a fever and is already planning ways to turn my beef roast into bile at the supper table."

"You're fired," Jacob said through his teeth.

"Well, I won't go, so there," Janet shot back. "You shut your mouth and stop throwing orders at me, young man. I used to put diapers on you when you were five feet shorter than you are now!"

"For God's sake, stop reminding me," he retorted, carrying Kate inside the dark hall. "Don't we have a light in this hall, or are you on another conservation binge?"

"Waste not, want not," Janet replied smugly, "and don't trip with Miss Kate."

He muttered something that Janet couldn't hear and Kate flushed.

He walked off down the hall to one of the guest rooms on the ground floor, just two doors down from his own room. At least, Kate imagined it was still his room. It had the same heavy antique furniture that he'd been using when Kate had visited Margo so many years before.

"We hardly use the upstairs anymore," he commented as he put her down on a spotless powder-blue coverlet under a canopied bed. "It's cold as hell in winter and too hard for Janet to go up and down when she has to clean it. We try to save her legs when we can, despite the fact that we ought to stand her up against the fence and shoot her."

"You'd miss her," Kate chided.

He leaned over her, his hands beside her head, his dark eyes piercing. "Maybe. How's the rib?"

"Just a little sore," she said softly. He was so good to look at. Involuntarily, her eyes ran over his hard face, tracing every line of it.

He saw the helpless pleasure in her expression and found himself smiling gently at her obvious delight in looking at him. He hadn't realized how exciting it could be to know that Kate loved him.

He bent a little and threatened her mouth with the minty warmth of his own, watching her eyes dilate and half close, watching her lips part for him. Yes, she wanted his mouth. He nuzzled her nose with his, hearing her breathing change in the stillness of the room. His own was quickening. It aroused him to feel her immediate response.

Because it did, he drew back, frowning a little. He had to keep things in perspective. Kate was here to heal, and he was providing for her out of guilt. Wasn't he? He blinked at his own confused reactions.

"Rest for a bit," he said, rising. "We'll have something to eat directly. I've got to sit down with my father and see what's happened while I've been away. Tom can keep you company."

"Of course. I don't need to be entertained, you know," she added with a faint smile.

"You don't need to be left alone to brood, either," he replied. He let his eyes wander down the length of her body, which was elegant in a pale gray pantsuit with a green ruffled blouse. She was pretty when she dressed up, and her body tormented him with memories. He remembered it in the first tentative seconds of passion, remembered it twisting softly under him, her moans quickly arousing him to that unexpected loss of control. His body tautened with the memory of a fulfillment so staggering, it still haunted him.

"Do you still like mystery novels?" she asked unexpectedly.

His eyebrows shot up. "Of course."

"I do, too. Do you have some new ones I could read while I'm here?"

"I've got dozens that I've acquired since your last visit," he replied. "You're welcome to borrow them."

"Thanks."

"Janet says one of your men wants to see you," Tom interrupted, smiling at Jacob as he brought in Kate's suitcase. "Something about some barbed wire that didn't come."

"Great," Jacob muttered. "I leave for a few days and the whole damned spread falls apart."

He went out, still muttering, and Tom exchanged wry grins with Kate. "Just like old times, isn't it?" he asked. "Jacob's more like his old self since Margo's wedding."

Kate didn't comment. "Sit down and talk to me," she said instead. "We haven't really had a chance to visit since you came over from New York." She settled back against the pillows with a weary sigh. "Tell me about your job."

He did, and went on to keep her in stitches with tales about his boss. His stories passed the time, and he kept on talking until Kate dozed off. He watched her, his green eyes worried. Kate had been odd lately—ever since Margo's wedding. He felt that her present state had something to do with Jacob, and that what happened had been more than a simple argument. But even though he loved her, he knew that she wouldn't welcome his interference. With a sigh, he got up and covered her with a quilt. Poor Kate, he thought. Her life had gone from bad to worse lately. And being around Jacob, considering her passion for him, was going to be more torment for her. He wondered why in the world she'd agreed to come here. He wished he and Jacob were friendly enough that he could ask. There were so many mysteries between his sister and Jacob. He hoped she wasn't going to let herself in for any more heartache than she'd already had.

Eight

Tom stayed two days, just long enough to see Kate settled; then he had to go back to work. At first she was lonely, but Janet made time to talk to her. Somehow Jacob was always early or late for meals, so that Kate had them with Hank and Janet. She didn't know if that was by accident or design on Jacob's part. He'd been acting strangely ever since her arrival, as if he were deeply regretting his impulse to bring her to the ranch to recuperate. Feeling a sense of tension, Kate made a point of staying out of his way. She knew he didn't have much free time, anyway, since it was fall. He and his men were busy getting the cattle to winter pasture, selling calves, moving out culls, moving in replacement heifers, checking for disease, tagging, doing all the hundred-and-one things that raising cattle required from season to season.

Her doctor in Chicago had made Jacob promise to have his own physician examine Kate forty-eight hours after they arrived in South Dakota, just to make sure no damage had been done. Jacob kept his word, and Dr. Wright checked Kate to make sure her broken rib was mending properly. She was still a little sore, but nothing like the way she had been those first few days. They'd removed the staples just before she left the hospital, and the rib belt, oddly enough, didn't hurt the stitches or the small incision where the drainage tube had been in her side. She was told to come back on the fourth week after surgery to have more X rays done, and if they were all right, she could dispense with the rib belt. At least, she thought ruefully, it no longer hurt to cough or sneeze or laugh, so she had to be getting better.

Hank had ridden into Blairsville with them to see the doctor, so there hadn't been any opportunity for Kate and Jacob to talk. Perhaps Jacob had wanted that, because he seemed reluctant to spend any time with her.

Of course, Kate hadn't expected to see much of Jacob, and she didn't complain about his absences. But at the end of her first week on the ranch, he came into her room unexpectedly as she was halfheartedly watching a television comedy special from the easy chair by the window.

He was wearing denims and a blue-checked western shirt, and his boots were still dusty from working. He smiled at the picture she made in her pale blue caftan, curled up in the pink chair with her feet bare.

"Are you watching that?" he asked, nodding toward the screen.

"Sort of," she said and smiled. "I'm okay. You don't have to entertain me. I don't want to get in the way."

She always put his comfort first, he thought with faint irritation. She wouldn't intrude on his privacy for anything, not even to ask about those books she wanted to

read. Since she'd been at Warlance, she'd kept very much
to herself, not bothering anyone. He felt a bit uncomfortable around her, and he'd made sure they weren't
alone for any length of time. She didn't seem to mind his
absence, and ironically, he found that frankly annoying.
He'd been working hard; he hadn't had a spare minute to
entertain her. But he felt guilty all the same, and her sac-
rificial attitude caught him on the raw. Any other woman
would have demanded attention, been petulant and insistent and haughty about it.

"Don't you ever get tired of sainthood?" he asked
unexpectedly, because he was tired and worn and impatient with her lack of spirit. "My God, all you need is a
halo!"

The attack surprised her. She hadn't expected him to
take off the gloves until she was well, but perhaps her
very presence in the house angered him. His conscience
was obviously bothering him since he found out the truth
about her past, and having to see her every day was only
adding to his sense of guilt.

She looked up at him quietly. "I should never have
come," she said then. "You haven't changed one bit.
You're about as thrilled to have me here as you'd be with
a toad in the house." She got to her feet slowly, because
she was weak and her side was still a little sore, but she
faced him squarely. "I hate to even ask it, but will you
please get me a ticket on the next bus out of here? Fail-
ing that, I'll call Tom."

The situation was getting out of hand too quickly. He
hadn't realized she'd take him at face value, but he
should have remembered her obsession with not imposing.

"I'm tired," he said shortly. "I'm short-tempered and
ill and I want to bite somebody. You were handy."

She stared at him unblinking, startled by the blunt admission.

"When I want you to leave, I'll say so," he snapped. His eyes darkened at the sight of her in that witchy blue caftan. He didn't think she was wearing anything under it, and that disturbed him even more.

"Excuse me, I thought you were asking me to leave," she said in a subdued tone.

He moved forward with a rough sigh and took her gently by the arms, easing her back down in her chair. He knelt in front of her and looked into her wounded eyes.

"Either you've forgotten, or you don't know," he began softly, "but I'm not an easy man to get along with. I have a black temper and I'm not shy about using it. If you don't learn to stand up to me, you're going to have one hell of a time trying to stay here."

"I don't want to fight," she said miserably. "I'm weak as a kitten, I miss my job and my brother, and I've got too much time to think."

He hadn't considered that. Her admission took the starch out of him all at once. "You've been keeping to yourself ever since Tom left," he reminded her. "I didn't know if you were shy, or just preferred your own company." He touched the arm of her chair idly. "Kate, I like being by myself. It's a hard habit to break. If you want to talk, I'll listen. If you want to be with me, all you have to do is say so."

Her eyes closed on a wave of embarrassment. "I don't need company, thank you," she said proudly. "Except that I'll have to ask you to get someone to drive me to the doctor next Friday for those X rays." And he could make what he liked of that; she wasn't going to beg him to spend any time with her.

"Talk about pride," he mused, watching her. "I thought I had a monopoly on it. You'd damned well rather crawl there than ask me to take you, wouldn't you?"

Her eyes opened, glaring. "You know I would," she whispered, and at the moment, she meant it. She felt an almost primitive dislike of him and the hold he had over her emotions.

It was going to be more difficult than he'd thought. She was as proud as he was, and she wasn't about to let down her guard. Not after what he'd done to her. It was going to be like pulling teeth just to get her to talk to him. Love was one thing. Trust was something else again. She might worship him from afar, but he was just beginning to understand that she was trying her best to shut him out, to keep him at arm's length.

"Why don't you come and keep me company while I do the book work?" he asked unexpectedly.

She stared at the screen. "I'd rather watch this. But thank you anyway."

He moved around her and switched the television off.

"Jacob!"

He ignored her protest. He bent and lifted her gently in his arms, careful not to jar her, and carried her out of the room and down the hall to his study. She was thinner than he remembered, and frankly delicate. He didn't want to know how much she weighed now. The wound and his treatment of her had taken their toll.

"You're as tight-lipped as I am, and about half as proud. You won't give an inch, and neither will I. You're not going to hole up in that room and shut me out. I didn't bring you here to watch you hibernate."

She felt his strength as he put her down on his burgundy leather sofa. She couldn't imagine that she'd really heard him say that, and her eyes mirrored her surprise.

"I thought you liked being alone," she said absently.

"So did I." He stood up and looked at her. Her hair was growing. Janet had helped her wash it, and it was clean and soft and shining.

"I need a robe...."

"Why?" he asked quietly. "Hank's playing poker with one of his friends, and Janet's gone home for the night. We're by ourselves. There's no one to see you except me."

Her face colored delicately. He cocked an eyebrow.

"You aren't shy?" he asked. "You don't have anything I haven't already seen."

The color grew worse. She averted her shamed eyes from him to the waxed floor with its Indian rugs.

"I'm sorry," he said tightly. "That was the last thing I should have said to you."

The apology helped, but she couldn't raise her eyes. He was bringing back too many painful memories.

He eased down on the sofa beside her, his dark eyes on her head. "I've never been so wrong about one human being in all my life," he said. "I wish you could have talked to me about it."

Her arms felt chilled. She folded them, staring at the rug. "It was too painful to talk about," she said. "My father was unbalanced. We knew it, but we were so little, Jacob. There was nothing we could do, no one we could turn to. By the time he died, we were... horribly scarred, mentally."

"And physically?" he probed, his jaw clenching as he remembered what Tom had told him about the circumstances of her father's death.

She dug her nails into her arm. "And physically," she said through her teeth. "Didn't you see the scars that day at the pool house?"

"I didn't see anything but red," he replied. "My God, I could have killed that boy!"

She looked up, shivers of pure pleasure going through her at the fiery darkness of his eyes. "He was only trying to help. You know how afraid I was of snakes. And I'd already made you suspicious by the way I kissed him." She lowered her eyes to the opening of his shirt, where thick black hair was visible against tanned skin. "You were playing tag with that Dugan woman...."

And Kate had been jealous. His heart raced with the knowledge. It explained a lot of things. He wanted to question her, to bring her feelings out into the open. But that wouldn't do. He didn't want her to know that he was aware of her feelings.

"She was playing tag with me," he replied casually. "I like Barbara. I always did." He pushed back a lock of her hair that had fallen over one eye. "She's engaged, did I tell you? To the Hardy man she always fancied."

Her heart skipped. "Is she?"

"Yes, she is. So if you'd planned on marrying me off to her, you're out of luck. I guess I'll just stay a bachelor."

"Then who'll inherit Warlance?"

He studied her blushing cheeks, drinking in the scent of roses that clung to her slender body. "Good question. I've only thought about children in recent years. I'm thirty-two. Eventually I'll have to marry, if I want an heir."

"I don't imagine you'll have any trouble finding a candidate," she said, avoiding his stare. Certainly not, she thought bitterly. The line would form at the gates and Jacob would be wined and dined and hunted like a fox.

"Won't I?" He leaned back, one arm behind her, his lean body elegant in its relaxed position. "I'm rich, Kate."

"So?" she replied, glancing at him.

"How will I know I'm not getting a gold digger?"

"Give it all away," she whispered conspiratorially.

He smiled faintly. "I'm not that desperate."

"Then you'll never know." Her gaze traveled over him, and she forced herself to look away before her eyes betrayed her.

She didn't know that they already had. Jacob's chest swelled with the knowledge that she wanted him. Her soft eyes had been shyly covetous, running down his body like hands. She could arouse him just by looking at him that way. He pursed his lips, wondering if she was even aware of the effect she had on him.

"When did you know you weren't pregnant?" he asked unexpectedly.

She went hot all over, and mumbled, "The next week."

His dark eyes searched her averted features. "I sweated it out, too," he said. "I knew you wouldn't talk to me, or want to see me. I called Tom and fed him some wild story about wanting to talk to both of you, just so he'd come down from New York and run interference for me. I had to know if there was going to be a child."

She gritted her teeth. "Well, there isn't, so you needn't worry."

"I'm not sure that I was worried," he mused quietly, touching her caftan where a fold of it rested on the sofa. "I wanted to know, that's all."

"I wouldn't have told you," she said.

He knew that, now. She'd have protected him even in that kind of circumstance. His dark gaze lifted and caught her wide green eyes. "Oh, but I'd have found out, Kate. Just the possibility of it would have kept me ten steps behind you until I knew one way or the other."

"And if...?" she probed hesitantly.

"You know me well enough that you don't even have to ask," he replied.

She lowered her eyes to his jeans, where the fabric lovingly traced the powerful muscles of his thighs. "You'd have married me."

"A man will do most anything when there's a child involved, if he has any sense of honor at all," he reminded her. He didn't add that the thought of having a child with Kate didn't bother him one bit. In fact, he'd felt vague disappointment when he'd learned that she wasn't pregnant. That had puzzled him. He couldn't equate that disappointment with desire. And it was only desire that he felt. Wasn't it?

"Well, it's a good thing it turned out this way," she said wearily, leaning her head back with her eyes closed. "I don't want to participate in any shotgun weddings. I'm not even sure I want children at all."

"Why?" he asked, shocked.

"They make people do crazy things," she said, remembering her father's cruelty.

"You can't judge all parents by yours," he began.

"Why not? You judge all women by your mother," she replied, turning her head to study him.

He started to speak and then closed his mouth, brooding for several seconds. "I do, don't I, Kate," he agreed after a little while.

"That must have been hard on you."

"Do you remember your mother?" he asked, evading her question.

She shook her head, and her eyes hardened. "Just bits and pieces. Mostly what my father said about her. She was a tramp. She ran off with another man and deserted Tom and me." Her lower lip trembled. "He beat me...!"

"Oh, God," he breathed, finding the thought unbearable. Frowning with something like pain, he reached for her, bringing her with exquisite tenderness across his lap to cradle her against him. "Oh, God, honey...!"

The comforting was sweet and heady, and she cried into the slow, pulsating warmth of his throat, clinging with her good arm because she couldn't lift the other without pain.

"I hated my mother," she wept. "I still do. How could she leave us? How could she?"

He smoothed her hair, nuzzling it with his hard cheek. "I don't understand parents any better than you do," he said quietly. "My mother ran off and left us without a word, and Hank never tried to find her or bring her back. I asked him why once, and he said that you can't make people stay with you if they don't want to. It sounded like a cop-out at the time, but the older I get, the better I understand it. In a way, he was saving us all more heartache."

"You never forgave her, did you?"

His hand stilled on her hair. "She was on her deathbed," he said softly. "And after all the pain, she was still my mother. Yes, Kate. I forgave her. And that's something I've never even told Hank."

She moved her face softly against his throat, feeling proud that he was willing to share something so personal with her. "I don't think I could have been that generous," she whispered. "I'll never forgive mine."

"Do you know where she is?" he asked.

She shook her head. "I've never had the money to try and trace her. I don't think I would even if I could. Tom and I suffered so horribly because of her. At least Hank was good to you."

"That he was, the old devil. We fight, but I'd die for him, you know."

She smiled. "I know."

It was nice, holding her in the silence of the room, hearing the wind outside beginning to cool the air. She fit against him so perfectly, and he remembered vividly how it felt to hold her with no fabric between them. Her breasts were pushing against his chest, and she was wearing only the light caftan over them. He could feel her nipples, taut with arousal, stabbing into the hard muscles of his chest, and his hand contracted in her hair.

She felt his sudden movement with faint curiosity, and drew her head back to look into his dark eyes.

"What is it?" she whispered.

He started to tell her what it was, but he wondered if she even realized that her breasts were telling him intimate secrets about her innermost desires. He sighed heavily and eased her back onto the sofa before he got to his feet and moved away. "Nothing, honey," he said. "I've got to get on my books. What would you like to read?"

"One of those new mysteries," she suggested, curious about his sudden withdrawal. Did he find her distasteful now?

He pulled down one of the big hardcover books and handed it to her. "Want me to tell you who the murderer is?" he asked with a faint grin.

"You do, and I'll throw something at you."

"Not with your left arm, you won't." He frowned as she moved and he saw the smoothness under that caftan. "Kate, are you wearing the rib belt?"

"The doctor said I didn't have to at night," she reminded him.

"I didn't jar you when I carried you in here?"

That seemed to concern him, and it made her feel vulnerable and very feminine. "No. I'm fine."

He nodded and went to sit behind his desk with a pencil and several pages of figures spread out in front of him. Kate tried to read, but it was so exciting just to sit and watch Jacob as he worked. His hair was very thick, almost black, and it gleamed in the overhead light. His hands were lean and dark and strong, very long-fingered, and his wrists had a faint covering of dark hair on their backs. His arms were long and muscular, straining against the soft fabric of his shirt. The shirt itself was unbuttoned at the throat, and the exciting glimpses she got of hair-covered tanned flesh were wildly arousing. His chin was strong, very stubborn. She smiled, letting her eyes run up from it to his firm, sensuous mouth with its thin upper lip and slightly fuller lower one, a mouth chiseled like that of a Greek statue. His nose had a crook in it; he used to be in fights all the time in his youth. And his eyes . . .

She flushed, because his eyes were staring right back at her, faintly amused by her uninhibited scrutiny.

"Enjoying yourself, Kate?" he asked humorously, and then could have bitten his tongue off at the flaring embarrassment on her face.

"I'm sorry. I didn't mean to stare at you." She looked doggedly down at the book without seeing a single word in it.

Jacob drew in a slow breath, hating his own blatant mockery. He hadn't meant to make fun of her feeling for him. It was just the way she looked at him. It had a strange, disturbing effect on his body. Everything about her did, lately. He'd worked himself into a stupor for no other reason than to slow down the feverish hunger she aroused, to fight the fire. She didn't know how often he lay awake reliving that night they'd spent together. She'd given him a kind of fulfillment he'd never had with anyone else, a shuddering completion that could knock the breath out of him just in memory.

He started to speak, but she seemed involved in the novel. He turned his attention back to his books, forcing himself not to look at her again. That caftan was the most seductive garment he'd ever seen her in. She probably thought it was concealing and proper attire. Actually, she could only have aroused him more by going stark naked.

It was hard for Kate to concentrate after that mocking remark of his. She felt self-conscious, afraid even to look up at him. Her old self would have been more than able to stand up to him, but she was weak and tired and there had been more nightmares than she wanted to admit. She could close her eyes and hear the sound of the bullets, feel the sudden, horrible impact of the bullet that had hit her, feel the unbearable pain that never seemed to end.

She closed her eyes with a faint shudder. Reporting had been a dream job before this happened. Now she was afraid. Afraid of what she might be expected to do. She realized that the accident was a freak—one of those things that happened one time out of several thousand, but her nerve was shattered. She was only just realizing that she couldn't go back to police reporting. That meant that if there wasn't another slot open at the paper—and they didn't have a large turnover—she might not have a job to go back to. Her check came regularly, once a week, and that was nice of Mr. Winthrop. The paper had insurance that would pay her hospital bill. But she was going to have to have a job, and what if there wasn't one available?

"What's wrong?" Jacob asked quietly.

She hadn't realized that he was watching the drift of expressions across her face. She forced a smile. "Nothing. I was just figuring out who the murderer is."

"Sure. With the book upside down."

She glanced down. Sure enough it was. She righted it, fumbling a little because she'd been caught.

He put down his pencil with a sigh and came around the desk. "Kate, you can't spend your life looking back."

She wouldn't meet his eyes. "I realize that."

"In no time at all, this will all be a bad dream."

She set the book aside and slowly got to her feet. "I'd like to go back and lie down. I think I can sleep now. Thanks for the company."

He stopped her before she got three feet, his hands strong and gentle on her arms. She could feel his warm breath in her hair.

"Talk to me."

She stiffened under his hands. "I'm all right. I don't need to confess anything, thanks."

He sighed heavily. Nothing was working out as he'd expected. She was every bit as zealous about privacy as he was. "I'm not used to other people, either. I talk to no one, least of all Hank, about things that bother me. I keep everything in." His fingers pressed her arms slightly, caressing. "This is as hard for me as it is for you. If you keep pulling back, we'll never be able to communicate with each other."

"I'm afraid of you," she said quietly.

"I'm not blind. I realize that. You've got every reason to feel that way, after what's happened. You let your guard down with me, and I betrayed you. That's going to take a lot of forgetting." He drew her slowly back until she was pressed against his warm chest, and his cheek nuzzled her clean, soft hair, making her heartbeat run wild. "I told you in the hospital that I've never tried to be gentle. It was the truth. Even with women, in intimacy..." His hands smoothed down her bare arms under the caftan. "I can't sleep at night anymore, remembering how I hurt you," he said under his breath. "I've avoided you ever since we got here, because I can't bear being reminded..."

She turned, curious. "Jacob, you didn't shoot me," she said.

"I pushed you in front of the gun," he replied, his eyes narrow and dark and haunted. "You were looking for a way out."

She turned beet red under that knowing stare. Her eyes fell to his chest, to its strong, quick rise and fall. "Police reporting can be dangerous in a city the size of Chicago," she said finally. "I thought it would help me to stop thinking about...what happened. I wasn't consciously trying to commit suicide."

"You don't know how I've blamed myself."

"You didn't know." She lifted soft, tender eyes to his. "I wanted you," she whispered shyly.

"I wanted you, too," he said quietly. He touched her hair, brushing it back, his dark eyes curiously soft in the silence of the room. "God help me, Kate, I still do."

Her heart ran wild. Just to hear him admit it in that deep, slow voice was enough to increase her pulse rate. She watched his face come closer, his eyes fall to her soft mouth. Her breath caught; being close to him was exquisitely sweet.

He saw the expression on her face and it aroused him unbearably to know how much pleasure she felt when he came close. His heart felt like a drum inside him as he brushed his hard mouth across her soft one.

"Kate," he groaned when he felt her immediate response. He drew her gently against him and his mouth opened.

She let him kiss her, drowning in the sweetness of being near him, being wanted by him. If this was all he could ever give her, it would be almost enough.

She moaned softly at the gentle penetration of his tongue inside the sweet darkness of her mouth, at the achingly tender caress of his fingers just under her arms as they moved with delicate precision toward her breasts.

Without any sense of self-preservation, she drew back to give him total access to her body.

"This is so sweet with you," he whispered huskily against her mouth as his thumbs found just the outer edges of her breasts and began to trace the swell. His mouth nuzzled hers, and he felt like flying, his powerful body vibrating with a totally new kind of pleasure.

Kate couldn't speak at all. His hands were arousing her to a fever of passion. She wanted him to touch her. She looked up at him, adoring him with her eyes as his mouth taunted hers.

He smiled tenderly at her open hunger. It amazed him that she could still welcome him after the way he'd treated her. Love, he thought dazedly, must be a powerful thing, to forgive so much. He wanted to give her pleasure, whether he felt it or not. He wanted to adore her with his hands, his mouth, to know the sweetness of her body in satiation.

She tried to lift her arms around his neck and grimaced when the left one wouldn't move up without pain.

"Don't do that," he whispered, smoothing the aching muscles under her left arm. "You're not well enough to use that arm, even to hold me with it."

She was burning for him, aching. "Jacob," she breathed adoringly.

He brushed his mouth over her closed eyes. "I'll hold you," he whispered back, "but not too close. I don't want to hurt that rib."

One lean arm slid behind her, gently supporting her, and he looked down at the caftan as he slowly drew his thumb onto her breast and saw the peak clearly outlined under the silky fabric.

Kate could hardly breathe. That light, teasing touch was madly exciting. She rested her cheek against his broad shoulder, watching the play of emotion on his dark face as he touched her.

"I never gave a damn about this kind of love play before," he whispered. "My God, it's exciting."

She touched the lean fingers that were caressing her, fascinated by the pleasure they gave, her own hand trembling on them. "Yes."

His dark eyes lifted to search hers, sharing a new kind of intimacy with her. "Still afraid of me?" he whispered.

"Not . . . like this," she said shyly.

The tips of his fingers drew across the taut nipple and her breath caught. He watched her eyes, swelling with pride at the way she was reacting to such very light lovemaking. "Do you like it?"

Her body was trembling. "Yes."

As her co-workers had said, she was painfully honest, even when it must have bruised her pride. "I like it, too," he breathed. "I haven't touched a woman, in any way, since that night with you."

She found it difficult to talk at all. "Haven't...you?"

"I dream about you," he whispered, easing his mouth down against hers. "Night after lonely night, I dream about what you gave me...."

The words dissolved into an aching groan as he kissed her, and even that was different. There was tenderness in him now, along with an almost tangible desire.

She accepted his mouth as gently as she accepted the hand that slowly, surely, covered her breast. She made a soft sound under his mouth at the tiny consummation after the agony of longing his fingers had caused. Her own hand held his there, caressed it softly, savored the deep, aching pleasure of his touch on her body.

"Making love to you...gives me such pleasure," he whispered against her lips. His mouth opened, brushing lazily, softly over her own, deeply arousing. His knees felt weak, his body felt lighter than air, as if he could fly. His free hand slid into her thick hair, savoring its silkiness while his other hand grew gently insistent, his fingers tracing the hard peak, feeling her own fingers touching, coaxing.

"Jacob," she moaned. She caught his hand in hers, and he stopped, letting her lift it away.

"All right," he whispered. "I'll stop."

"No." Shyly, she drew his hand back to her body.

His body went rigid. He looked at her with an explosive kind of protectiveness surging inside him.

"No, sweetheart," he whispered tenderly. "No, not now."

She blushed, averting her face. She'd offered herself to him, and he'd rejected her just like he had before...

He tilted her chin up and made her look at him. "I want you," he said softly. "Right now there's nothing in the world I want more than to lie you down on that sofa and strip you and draw you under my body in passion." He shuddered at his own description, then drew himself up short. "But you've got a busted rib, little Kate, and for all that tenderness we just shared, I don't feel like being a gentle lover right now." He bent, crushing his mouth roughly against hers. "I feel like that, Kate," he breathed as his teeth nipped softly at her full lower lip. "I want to throw you down and ravish you...!"

Her breath caught. She clutched at his hard arms; the hunger for him was so strong.

"Yes, you want that, too, don't you?" he asked huskily, watching her face. "Even after last time...."

"I came so close last time," she whispered, shaking. "So close, and I could almost touch the sun, and then it was over."

He seemed to stop breathing. He'd thought that she hated sex because of what he'd done to her; she'd even said that it was horrible... Of course, if she'd thought so, she wouldn't be letting him touch her now.

He framed her face in his hands. "Say that again," he whispered.

She felt shy and embarrassed all at once. "You heard me," she faltered.

"I hope I did," he breathed fervently, probing her eyes. "My God, you can't imagine how it hurt my pride when you said it was 'horrible....'"

Her lips fell open. She hadn't even considered his point of view. Her face colored, but she didn't lower her eyes. "Oh, Jacob, no...I didn't mean...I felt empty. All that hunger, and I felt that there should have been something more, and there wasn't. It was kind of like a sneeze that backs up..." She smiled self-consciously and then she did lower her eyes. "I wanted to explain, but it was so difficult. I didn't understand what was happening to me."

"Oh, my God," he whispered. He drew her against him, protective, his hands holding her head, cradling it to his chest. He closed his eyes. "So that was it." He nuzzled his face against her soft hair. "I should have known, but when I realized how innocent you were, I wasn't surprised that it might have seemed horrible. A man in the throes of passion isn't the best kind of partner for a virgin."

"You wouldn't have been that way if I hadn't pushed you," she admitted. "I'd read all those things I did in a big, sexy novel, and when the heroine did it, the hero was rather reserved and slow..."

He actually laughed. "No wonder they call it fiction," he mused.

"I didn't want you to stop," she whispered. "I knew if you thought I was a virgin, you'd go away and I'd never see you again."

"You'd have seen me again, all right. Or didn't you realize that I was just as attracted to you as you were to me?"

"Not at the time," she replied. She sighed, content to stand forever in his gentle embrace.

"Are you all right?" he asked.

"I'm happy."

He realized with a start that he was, too. Happiness wasn't something he normally contemplated. He enjoyed life well enough; he liked his work. But happiness... He looked down at the dark head so trusting against his broad chest and felt flooded with contentment. She made him feel protective and tender and ablaze with passion. An odd mixture to be aroused by a little virgin.

That amused him, and he chuckled softly. "I'm tired," he said. He kissed her hair. "And you should be, even if you aren't. I'm going to carry you back to bed, and then I'm going to turn in, too. The book work can wait. It's been a damned long day."

She felt vague disappointment. It had been so sweet to stand in his embrace. "You don't have to carry me...." she began.

He lifted her gently, smiling at her. "Yes, I do. I like carrying you. It makes me feel manly and strong and macho and all those other descriptive words that men aren't supposed to feel in our enlightened society."

He started off down the hall and she laughed gently, sighing. "I like being carried," she admitted. "It makes me feel feminine and protected and vulnerable and all those other descriptive words that women aren't supposed to feel when they're liberated."

"I guess you and I are throwbacks to another age, Kate."

"I expect so." She closed her eyes, savoring the strength of his arms, the masculine scent of him as he carried her down the long hall into her room, and laid her on the bed.

He bent over her, his hair slightly mussed, his shirt open at the throat, his body powerful in that arched position, his dark eyes glittering down at her. "Lucky girl," he murmured wickedly, "to have a broken rib at such a convenient time."

She smiled up at him. As protective as he'd suddenly become, she didn't think it likely that he'd take advantage of her. "Thank you for bringing me back here," she murmured. "I hope you sleep well."

He bent and brushed his mouth over her forehead carelessly. "If you wake up frightened, come find me. I'll take you in with me for the rest of the night."

"Oh, you couldn't . . . !"

"No one would know, Kate," he said quietly. "Hank sleeps until eight, and Janet doesn't do the bedrooms until noon. I'd make sure you were in your own bed before I got ready to leave. And nothing would happen, despite the way I've teased you tonight," he added firmly. "I've made one big mistake with you. I'm not going to compound it by adding another seduction to the list."

And how was she supposed to interpret that, she wondered as he turned out the light, smiled at her, wished her good-night and shut the door.

She closed her eyes with a sigh and found that she was, after all, pretty sleepy. But somewhere in the middle of the night, machine guns started firing all around her and she screamed, sitting straight up in the darkness with terror choking her.

Nine

The door opened seconds later, and the light went on. Jacob was beside her in an instant. Apparently he'd been to bed, because he was wearing navy-blue pajama bottoms and nothing else. His broad chest was sensuously bare, as she'd rarely seen it, rippling with darkly tanned muscle and thick hair that ran in a wedge down past his pajama trousers.

"Nightmare?" he asked gently, studying her pale, tear-stained face.

"Yes. The gun..." She put her face in her hands. "Oh, Jacob, will they never stop?"

"One day, I expect. Come on."

He moved the covers aside and lifted her gently against his broad, hair-matted chest. She curled close, loving the spicy smell of his body, delighting in the feel of the thick hair under her cheek and her free hand.

"Don't do too much of that," he murmured with black humor as he turned out her light and closed the door on his way back to his own room with her.

"Hmm?" she asked drowsily.

"Stroking my chest with that little hand," he whispered at her ear. "It arouses me."

"Oh." She stilled her fingers with a small laugh at her own ignorance. "Sorry."

"Yes. So am I." He carried her into his dark room and kicked the door shut behind them. "Hold on. Every time I get up in the night, the bed moves from where I left it."

She smiled at the admission, and sighed gently when he put her down on the sheets, which were still warm from his body. A second later he slid into the bed beside her.

"Come here," he murmured, drawing her head against his shoulder. "Just lie still and don't play with my chest, and everything will be fine."

"I've never slept with anyone before," she confessed drowsily.

"You slept with me," he reminded her.

"We didn't sleep."

He sighed heavily. "No, we didn't." He brushed his lips against her forehead. "Is it getting easier, that blight on your spotless conscience?" he asked gently.

"A little."

"Would it get easier," he asked, his voice deepening, "if we married?"

She wasn't sure she'd heard him at all. She stiffened a little in the darkness, aware of his warmth and strength and quick breathing beside her.

"Think about it, Kate," he said. "You might get used to the idea."

"I won't let you marry me out of guilt, Jacob," she said finally. "Marriage seems to be hard enough even when people love each other. And we don't," she added, forcing herself to tell the lie.

He knew it was a lie, of course. He smiled in the darkness, and touched her face. "Suppose I told you that I loved you," he asked, thinking how comfortable the words felt, even though he didn't quite mean them.

"Suppose you told me that Warlance was in Tibet," she said. She closed her eyes, wishing with all her heart that he could say those exquisite words and mean them.

"Aren't you tired of living alone?" he asked, changing tactics. "We could live together—like friends, if that's how you want it."

It would solve all her problems and create more at the same time. She didn't know how she could live with him and face the day-to-day anguish of hiding her true feelings while she got used to his indifference.

"No, Jacob," she said. "It wouldn't work. But thank you."

That caught him on the raw. He was trying to do the right thing, to ease her conscience, to take care of her, to make up for what he'd done. And she was throwing the offer back at him.

"Listen, honey, there are plenty of women who'd give their eyeteeth to marry me, even just for my money," he said curtly.

"So marry one of them," she replied, forcing her tone to be light and careless.

"Most women don't want a platonic marriage."

"Other women wouldn't, I expect," she faltered.

"I don't want other women," he said coldly, and then felt himself go rigid with the knowledge that it was the truth. He didn't want to look at anyone except Kate, much less go to bed with anyone else. "If I can't have you, I'll go without."

In the darkness, her own heartbeat sounded very loud. She stared at the dark ceiling. "I don't understand."

"Neither do I. Maybe I've got a guilty conscience. I don't go around seducing virgins. I hurt you, and remembering it hurts me. Maybe I've got a hang-up."

"You'll get over it."

"Will you?" he asked. He rolled over, looking down at her in the faint glow from the outside security lights. "Will you forget that night, as long as you live?"

"Well, no, but . . ."

"Will you ever want another man to make love to you?" he persisted.

"No." It sounded blunt, but it was the way she felt. "No, I couldn't let any other man touch me. Only you . . . that way."

His body burned with pride. Even though he'd hurt her, she hadn't stopped wanting him. She loved his touch, and he knew it, and it made him feel like a giant.

"Only me." He brushed his mouth over her closed eyes, and his hand smoothed down over her caftan, quickening her breathing as he touched her breasts and found their tips already hard and welcoming. "Someday, I'll take you right up to the sun in my arms, Kate."

"Ja . . . cob," she bit off.

He found the buttons under her arm, and unfastened them, enough to allow the slow, gentle intrusion of his hand onto bare flesh.

"Oh, God, you're soft, Kate," he breathed, sliding his fingers tenderly over her bare breasts. "Soft and exquisitely silky. Baby, you're so sweet to touch."

She moaned helplessly as her body turned to flame. Her good arm lifted. She found the buttons on the shoulder and fumbled them open and pulled the fabric completely aside.

"Yes," he whispered, feeling her hunger reflected in his own body. "Yes, I want it, too."

He moved her into the thin strip of light that filtered in through the window. "I want to see this sweet body," he said huskily. "I want to get drunk on the sight of you."

Her body trembled as she saw his eyes, felt his hands blatantly caressing her. His gaze went to her body, and she saw him smile at the wild reaction he coaxed from her as he teased the tips of her breasts.

"Lie still," he whispered, bending. "I don't want to hurt you. No, honey, don't start arching up toward my mouth. I'll give you what you want without any coaxing."

He kissed the swollen softness with tender lips, sliding his hands under her to support her, lift her. He heard her sharp, gasping little moans, and had to fight not to deepen the drugging intimacy. But he knew how delicate she still was. He couldn't have her, not yet. But he could make love to her in this exquisitely tender way. He could have those sweet little cries she'd never given to another man; he could touch her as no other hands ever had, or would.

It made him drunk with pleasure. In his passion, he nipped her, and she caught his head and made a frightened sound.

He lifted his chin to look at her, smiling down. "Men get carried away, remember?" he whispered. "You're silky and sweet under my mouth, and when I think about how virginal you are, I feel savagely male."

"You . . . bit me."

"Not hard enough to hurt," he whispered. "I never would. It's a kind of love play. A way of expressing passion."

"Oh." She stared at him, her eyes soft with love, wide with curiosity.

"Your upbringing scarred your emotions, I know. But will you try to remember that what we're doing together is part of life? That men and women were created to join, to become one in physical union?"

"Yes, but . . . but not in lust," she whispered.

He frowned faintly, his hands stilling. "Kate, do you think that all I feel for you is lust?"

She lowered her eyes to his broad, hair-matted chest, watching the ripple of muscle as he shifted over her. "Isn't it?"

He didn't know how to answer her. He was just realizing that what he felt wasn't physical alone. He wanted to please her. His own satisfaction didn't seem so important these days. He touched her face, loving the very structure of it, the softness of her skin. "No. I don't think it ever was. If I hadn't gone over the edge that night in your apartment, I'd have made sure you never wanted to forget what we did. I had these exquisite fantasies about loving you half to death."

Her heart jumped. How sweet that sounded. She looked up at him, her eyes so soft that he got lost in them. "I'm sorry about what I said to you . . ."

He brushed his mouth over hers. "Not half as sorry as I am about that damned hundred-dollar bill."

"I understand now."

"I could have lost you," he said under his breath. "The doctor said if that bullet had gone two inches lower, you'd have died."

"But it didn't, and I didn't," she reminded him. Her hands lifted to his chest, trembling a little at the delicious feel of all that muscle and its furry covering. "What did you say to me when you came into the intensive-care unit?''

"Things.''

She moved her hands softly, and he tensed. "What kind of things?''

He nuzzled her face with his. "Very personal ones, that I wouldn't repeat cold sober or in broad daylight. I'm rather glad that you don't remember hearing them.''

Now she really was curious. What could he have told her that he didn't want her to know? He was such a private person, so alone. But then, so was she.

"I think you pulled me back,'' she confessed. She looked at his chest, watched it ripple as she caressed it. "I didn't care about living.''

"That's what bothered me. You were close to the edge, and I'd given you every reason in the world to look for a way over.''

His breath caught as her hands moved again. He wavered between the need to let her caress him and the stupidity of not stopping her before things got any hotter than they already were.

"Kate . . . I really think that we'd better stop now.''

She looked at the rigidity of his chest and understood. With a deep sigh, she moved her hands to his arms instead. "What a pity, when I was just getting the hang of it,'' she murmured dryly, although her heart was going mad.

"I feel the same way. But you can't handle passionate lovemaking until that rib heals.''

She blushed. "No, I don't suppose so.''

"It would be passionate, too,'' he breathed, slowly fastening the caftan over her breasts. "I'm shaking like a teenage boy right now.''

She wondered if he'd ever admitted to that with any other woman. She almost asked, but she was too jealous of him to want the answer. She watched his dark face while he finished closing the buttons on her shoulder.

"Jacob, tell me what just happened wasn't out of guilt."

"Guilt?" He stared down at her for a long minute until, with a rigid smile, he moved onto his side and reached for her, pulling her gently against the length of him, his hands pressing her hips slowly against the unmistakable contours of his body. "Does this feel like guilt? Or are you still innocent enough to think a man can fake desire?"

Her legs felt trembly. She caught his hands, but he wouldn't release her. "I don't know a lot about it," she said.

"This," he emphasized, shifting her against him gently, "is a hell of a nuisance. I'm not usually stupid enough to encourage it unless I'm in a position to satisfy it. It's damned uncomfortable."

She was flaming by now. "Oh."

He released her and rolled over onto his back, arching a little as the ache increased before it finally began to subside. He forced himself to breathe normally, to relax.

"In the old days, about the time you decided to drive me crazy with Gerald what's-his-name, I could hear your voice on the phone and have that happen," he said quietly. "Of course, it's diminished a little over the years."

He sounded dry, and she sat up, staring down at him. Yes, he was smiling, just faintly.

"Now do you begin to understand what happened that night?" he asked, his voice deep and gentle. "I've wanted you for so many years that I dreamed about you all the time, and then there you were, wanting me back, and we were in bed together. A loaded gun wouldn't have stopped me."

"You wouldn't come near me, all those years," she said.

"I knew what would happen if I did," he replied. He drew her back down again, her head using his shoulder as a pillow. "There was Margo, and you were friends. I didn't want to have to explain to my niece why she couldn't play around with boys when I was playing around with her best friend."

"You wouldn't have played around with me after the first time," she reminded him.

He smiled, touching her hair gently. "That's true enough. It still makes me feel incredibly male, knowing that I was the first. I'm only sorry that I didn't give you the pleasure I felt."

She stared at the steady rise and fall of his chest. "Will we ever make love again?" she whispered, blurting it out.

"If you marry me, we will," he replied after a minute. "Otherwise, I don't think my conscience, or yours, will let us."

She had to fight tears. "That kind of marriage wouldn't work."

"Let it lie, for now. We'll plug along for a while and see how it goes." He brushed his lips across her forehead. "Sleep well."

"Are you all right now?" she asked softly.

He chuckled. "I'm all right." He drew the covers over them with a long sigh. "Curl up against me and we'll try to sleep."

He turned on his side and drew her back into the curve of his body, and she caught her breath at the delicious sensations it produced.

"Just try not to move around too much," he whispered into her ear.

She laughed, because she could feel why. It was magic, this closeness that had come so unexpectedly, this intimacy that was warm and sweet and tender. She sighed, linking her fingers into the hand that curved across her arm. He felt warm and strong at her back, and she knew there wouldn't be any more nightmares. Not this night. She closed her eyes, wishing that it could last forever.

But she awoke the next morning in her own bed, and at first it seemed that the night before had been a sweet dream. She sat up, and with the movement, she caught the spicy scent of Jacob's cologne still clinging to her. And beside her, on the next pillow, was a white rose, like the few roses still blooming on the bush outside the back door.

She picked it up and inhaled its dew-kissed fragrance, smiling softly to herself. No. It hadn't been a dream after all.

She put on her rib belt and got dressed, feeling young and extraordinarily happy. Jacob had asked her to marry him.

That didn't mean that he loved her, of course. But it had to be a start of some kind, if he'd been thinking about it.

In jeans, a loose green knit blouse, and boots, she went slowly down the hall and into the dining room. Hank was gone, but Jacob was still there, pushing eggs around on his plate absently.

He looked up when she walked in, and his eyes kindled as he smiled at her.

"Finally," he murmured. "I wondered how much longer I could push these damned cold eggs around on my plate without making Janet suspicious."

"Were you waiting for me?" she asked, returning the smile.

"What do you think?" he slid back his chair and stood up, holding out his hand. She took it and was drawn gently into his hard arms and kissed with warm, rough affection.

"Good morning," she whispered under his lips.

"Good morning yourself. Did you find the rose?"

She smiled. "Yes. Thank you."

He kissed her eyelids. "I wish your rib was healed, Kate, because I want you a hell of a lot closer than this."

"Me, too," she breathed. She could feel his heart beating against her breasts. "Did you sleep?"

"Eventually," he mused, drawing back. "I lay and looked at you for a long, long time before I finally did. We're going to have to get married, Kate."

She looked down at his chest. She wanted to say yes. She wanted him. But a tiny part of her knew that it would be disastrous. He might be feeling new things with her, but that didn't necessarily mean he loved her. He admitted himself that a great deal of what he felt was physical. That would wear off, when he was totally satisfied, and what would they have left?

"I can't marry you."

"Why?"

He sounded indignant. She met his dark eyes. "Jacob, desire isn't enough. Without love..."

"You love me, though, Kate," he said quietly, watching her face. "You always have."

She seemed to stop breathing. She searched his eyes. Was he guessing...?

"Tom told me everything, just before they took you to the hospital," he said. "I even saw the photos of me..."

Her reaction was unexpected. She tore away from him, wild-eyed, oblivious of the shock in his face and the pain in her rib.

"Well, my God, it's all right," he said shortly, because her actions surprised him. "There's nothing to be embarrassed about."

But there was. Kate was dying inside. She felt as if her soul had been stripped naked in front of an audience. She went alternately red and white, and then the tears started.

It was just too much to have Jacob know everything. What he felt had been pity; now she was sure of it. Pity and guilt, because she loved him and he'd hurt her, Now he was trying to make up for that hurt, and she'd believed that he was just beginning to feel something for her. What a fool she'd been!

He started toward her, and she jerked back.

"No," she whispered tearfully. "No, don't you ever touch me again. I don't want your pity, Jacob!"

She turned and ran down the hall into her room, closing the door and locking it behind her. She didn't even hear him knock, or try the doorknob, and after a minute he called her name.

She ignored him, falling onto the bed in tears. She didn't know what she was going to do, but she couldn't stay at Warlance. Outside, thunder rattled the house and lightning struck toward the ground as the storm brought wind and pelting rain. Kate closed her eyes, grateful for the noise that drowned out Jacob's voice. She pulled the pillow over her head to make sure she couldn't understand. He sounded coaxing, then demanding and, finally, furiously angry. The sound of his boots stalking off down the hall was loud enough to penetrate through the pillow. With a sob, she buried her face and cried until her chest was sore again.

Ten

___

Kate spent the rest of the morning in her room, not leaving it until she was certain that Jacob had gone out. Then she sat in the living room, trying to decide what to do. It was raining outside, and she thought about the cowboys out in the chilly, wet weather. She thought about Jacob, and felt her heart go cold.

Why had he admitted that Tom had told him? Was it because she'd refused to marry him, and he'd been irritated when she didn't jump at the chance? Did he think that she was so selfish that she'd marry him just because she wanted it, without any thought for what it would be like for him? Being tied to a woman he didn't love would make him miserable for the rest of his life. Loving sometimes required sacrifices, but apparently he didn't know that.

One thing was certain; she had to get away from here. She couldn't bear the embarrassment of being around

Jacob and knowing that she had no secrets from him. Her eyes closed as she relived the sweetness of the night before. The memory turned bitter when she realized that pity had motivated him. He knew that she loved him. That slow, tender loving had been because he thought it would please her, just another way of making restitution for the hurt he'd dealt her in Chicago. Maybe he wanted her, too, but she knew it hadn't been out of love, and that was what hurt the most.

The tears came again, pouring down her cheeks. She had to go back to Chicago. But if she did, what was she going to do? She knew she couldn't work for another week or so at least, and even then, doing police news was going to be impossible. She was drawing her paycheck, but that would run out when her recuperation period was over. She had pitiful little savings. So what was she to do? She didn't feel right about imposing on Tom, although she knew he'd come for her if she called him.

She was still worrying about the future when Hank came in, tossing off his yellow slicker, muttering under his breath. He glanced at Kate and grinned sheepishly.

"Sorry, I got carried away. My son," he said, nodding toward the front door, "is out there in his shirtsleeves, getting drenched, and the temperature is dropping. So naturally I asked him did he want a raincoat. He said some words I won't repeat and stomped off mumbling something about hoping he catches his death." He frowned. "Did the two of you get into another argument or something, Katie?"

He was the only person who ever called her by that nickname. She shifted restlessly on the sofa. "Well . . . kind of."

"Kind of?"

She grimaced. "Jacob asked me to marry him and I said no." She noted the shock on his face. "Well, he doesn't love me, Hank," she said. "It wouldn't be right."

He whistled. "I never thought I'd live to see the day he'd propose to any woman. Now the miracle has happened, and you have to go all righteous and say no. Are you crazy?" he asked. "My gosh, girl, I'm sixty years old. If he doesn't get a move on, I'll never have grandkids. And you're a nice girl. We all know and like you—he couldn't do better if he looked for years." He sat down across from her. "See here, Kate, you need to think about this."

"I have thought about it." She blushed, lowering her eyes. "I love him, and he knew all the time—Tom told him. Jacob blurted it out this morning when I said I wouldn't marry him, and I'm so hurt ...!"

She was crying and Hank felt awkward. He patted her hand gently. "Now, now," he said, grimacing. "Now, now."

"I want to leave," she whispered. "But I've got nowhere to go."

"He'd just come after you if you left," he said reasonably. "Jay don't give up when he sets his mind to something, you know. That is, if he don't kill himself working out in the pouring rain."

"Doctors say that you don't catch cold even in the rain unless you've been exposed to a virus or something," she said, more to reassure herself than to convince him.

"Yeah, but there's a virus going through the bunkhouse, one of those chest things with bronchitis. I sure hope he doesn't get it."

So did Kate, but she didn't know what to do. She couldn't even face Jacob right now, much less go out and start trying to tell him what to do.

"You might get one of the men to hit him over the head and drag him back here," she suggested as she dabbed at the tears on her face.

"There's a thought. Are you okay now?"

She forced a smile. "I'm okay."

"Don't make such heavy weather of it. Everything will work out." He smiled. "Now go get some lunch and I'll go out and try to save Jay from himself."

"All right. You're a nice man, Hank."

"Why, sure I am," he agreed. "And you're a nice girl. Too bad we can't include Jay, but he ain't nice."

"Once in a while..." she protested.

"Maybe. Go on, now."

She got up and went off to find Janet. But if she expected Hank to get anywhere with his stubborn offspring, she was disappointed. Night came, and Jacob was still out. By the time she went reluctantly to bed, he hadn't put a foot in the door.

The next morning, he was still at the table when she came down after a sleepless night. Her heart jumped. She'd expected him to be gone already.

She tried to find words, but couldn't. Having him know everything in her heart made her feel vulnerable and nervous.

It was too late to run. She pulled out a chair and sat down, glancing quickly at Jacob.

He was pale, and when he asked her to pass the bacon, his voice sounded hoarse.

"All that rain," she said hesitantly. "You've caught cold."

"Maybe I'll die," he shot back, glaring at her. "I hope if I do that I lie on your conscience like lead, Kate."

She flushed and pulled her eyes to the coffee she was pouring into her cup. "I didn't ask you to try and drown yourself."

"You won't marry me," he said coldly.

"You know why, too."

"I wish I could understand why women are so damned secretive about their feelings," he muttered. He put his fork down and glared at her. "What difference does it make if I know that you care about me? The world hasn't stopped turning, has it? The sky hasn't fallen on your head!"

"It's embarrassing!" she shot back.

"Why?"

She looked at him and away, stirring too much cream into her coffee while she tried to deal with the intimacy of the conversation. "I feel vulnerable."

"Maybe I do, too, Kate."

She laughed bitterly. "How could you? You don't care about me."

There was a long pause, and she looked up to find him watching her with eyes that looked strange, unusually dark. "I'm still in the learning stages about that," he confessed, his voice husky. He cleared his throat, and coughed. "Damned cold rain. I feel like hell."

"Why don't you go back to bed?" she ventured.

"Loving me doesn't give you the right to mother me," he replied curtly, and glared at her shocked expression. "I don't want to go to bed, thank you. I've got cattle to look after."

"You can't look after them if you die," she replied. Talking about her feelings was beginning to feel natural—at least with him it was.

"I won't die." He sipped his coffee, made a face at the eggs and bacon and stood up. "I can't eat. I'm going out."

But when he started to move, he swayed. Kate jumped up without thinking and got under his arm. His body felt hot, and when she reached up to feel his forehead, it was blazing.

"Jacob, you've got a fever. A high one," she announced.

"I do feel a bit woozy. Here, now, honey, don't put that rib at risk. I can lean against the wall."

"Just lean on me. I won't let you hurt my rib," she protested. "Let's get you to bed."

"I haven't got time for this, Kate," he grumbled. But he went with her, feeling sick and hollow—and oddly elated because Kate loved him. It had hurt more than he wanted to admit, having her run from him because he'd blurted that out about her feelings. His feverish eyes looked down on her dark head. She was one in a million. And she was going to marry him, one way or the other. He wasn't letting her get away.

"Now, lie down while I get these off," she said when they were beside his bed. She watched him lie down, and reached for his boot.

"No, you don't," he replied, glaring at her. "You aren't supposed to do any lifting, or pulling, and boots don't come off without some work. Get Hank."

She sighed. He was right. "Okay. Where is he?"

"Probably at the barn. The vet was coming to check some new stock for us." Stretched catty-cornered over the coverlet, his hat off, his feet hanging off the mattress, he closed his eyes. He looked sick.

"I'll get him. You stay put."

He opened one eye. "Worried about me?" he asked, and grinned wickedly.

She glared. "It would serve you right if I ignored you."

He closed the eye again. "No, it wouldn't. It feels good, being loved," he said in a slow, tender voice, and he smiled.

She flushed, and tried to find the right words to reply. He was confusing her.

He opened his eyes to study her reaction, and the smile was still there, even more tender than before. "Put on a raincoat before you go out," he reminded her. "I don't want you to catch cold."

A warm glow grew inside her. She smiled back at him, fascinated by his unexpected tenderness. Then she quickly went out, a little afraid of his new attitude.

Hank came at once, and when he saw Jacob, he immediately phoned the doctor, who said to bring the patient in. Kate got him into a raincoat and they stuffed him into the cab of the pickup and drove him into Blairsville.

It was a bad case of bronchitis, with a viral infection aggravating it. The doctor gave Jacob an injection and prescriptions for antibiotics and a cough syrup. They picked up the prescriptions on the way home. Then Hank got him undressed and into bed, Janet made him chicken soup and Kate sat with him while Hank went out to work.

He slept most of the day. Kate watched him with loving eyes, enjoying the unique experience of being allowed to look at him without having to worry about being seen. Even pale and feverish, he delighted her hungry eyes.

She left him only long enough to eat a quick dinner and then went back to his bedside with a cup of coffee to keep her warm. By night, he was stirring.

"I feel worse now than I did when I got up," he murmured.

"Darkness before dawn," she said cheerfully.

He smiled at her. "I guess. You should be in bed."

"I'll go in a little while."

"If you're going to stay, how about reading me something?"

"What would you like to hear? One of those murder mysteries?"

"I'd rather hear market news. There's a recent cattlemen's association magazine on my dresser."

"Okay."

She got it and read him an article about new marketing techniques and a report on forage grasses.

"That reminds me," he murmured, "I've got the boys building a greenhouse for you. It should be finished in a day or so. Then we'll get you some pots and potting soil and some plant stock from the nursery in Pierre."

"You don't need to worry with that," she said, pleased that he'd remembered his promise, and sad that she wouldn't get to use the greenhouse. "I'll be able to leave in another week, you know," she added quietly.

He opened his eyes and looked at her, without any subterfuge or camouflage. "I want you where I am."

She flushed. "I have a job...."

"Quit it," he said.

The color grew worse. "Jacob, I—"

"I can support you. I've got a damned empire out here, except at tax time. We can live on beef for a while, even if the money gives out. You can grow things in the greenhouse and we'll have vegetables year-round."

He didn't sound as if he were joking. "You don't want to marry," she reminded him. "You've always said you didn't."

"I've said a lot of stupid things, Kate. Haven't you noticed?" He moved onto his side so that he could see her. "Listen, don't you want kids?"

"Well, yes," she admitted, her eyes lingering with hopeless longing on his dark face.

"My kids?" he persisted gently, smiling.

She averted her eyes. "I'll kill my brother," she said through her teeth.

"He's in New York, and I'll protect him. I told you, I like being loved. Nobody ever loved me before, except family."

Memories flashed through her mind. A deep, slow voice, faintly unsteady, whispering that. Her eyes widened, holding his. "You said that...you told me that when I was in the intensive care unit. You said, 'Don't die on me...'"

The smile faded, and he held her eyes relentlessly. "Yes. And I told you that I didn't think I wanted to live without you. Would you like to hear me say it again?"

"You were just overwrought," she said.

"I still am. I want you." He reached out and caught her hand gently in his. "Don't turn away like that. Wanting isn't some unforgivable sin. It's part of that emotion you don't want me to know you feel for me." He smiled at her softly. "Kate, you like planting things and watching them grow. Well, I guess God does, too. He arranged things so that a man and a woman do the planting, and the baby is the little seed that grows. Life is a miracle, Kate."

She searched his dark eyes quietly. "I was punished every time I smiled at a boy," she whispered. "All Tom and I heard was how sinful sex was."

"Your father was a sick man, honey," he said gently. "He was sick, and maybe he had more responsibility than he could handle."

"If my mother hadn't left us—"

He drew her hand to his mouth. "My mother left me, too," he reminded her. "It wasn't my fault when she left, any more than you were to blame for your mother's desertion. Maybe she had a reason. You were very young when she left. It's hard for a child to understand adult reasoning."

"I used to cry for her at night," she told him. "I missed her so much."

"Maybe she missed you and Tom, too." His eyes narrowed. He'd just had an idea, but he wasn't going to share it with Kate just yet. Not until he worked out the details.

Kate didn't answer. She looked at the lean, strong hand holding hers, and involuntarily her fingers stroked over the back of it.

"I wish I felt better," he murmured, watching her. "I want to make love to you."

She felt heat tingle through her. For an old-fashioned reactionary, he had a sexy way of talking to her. She felt naive with him.

"So shy," he mused, turning her hand over so that he could lock his warm fingers into hers. "And I've hurt you without even realizing how much, all these long years we've been apart. I wish I could take back every painful thing I've ever said to you."

"You said what you felt at the time. There's no need for any regrets," she replied quietly.

"Think so? Get my wallet off the dresser, honey."

Frowning, she found the battered black cowhide wallet and handed it to him. He struggled into a sitting position, knocking the covers off his broad, hair-matted chest, and opened the wallet. He thumbed through the plastic inserts to the one he'd shown Morgan Winthrop at the newspaper office. He turned it, and showed it to Kate.

She stared at the picture, dumbfounded. It wasn't something he'd just stuck in there to impress her. From the faded, wrinkled condition of it, and the age she was when it had been taken, he'd been carrying the photograph around for a lot of years. It was of her, at one of Margo's parties, in a Mexican skirt and peasant blouse, with her long hair settled around her bare shoulders and her mouth smiling at the photographer. There was a brilliance in that smile that puzzled her, until she remembered that Jacob had taken the picture for Margo, who'd been in it with her. He'd cut it to fit his wallet, removing Margo's image in the process.

"I never knew why you looked so beautiful until Tom told me the truth," he said, watching her rapt expression. "And then I realized that the light in your eyes in that picture was for me. I've carried it everywhere with me, for years. Having it with me made me feel at home wherever I happened to be." He reached out and took the wallet back from her, glancing warmly at the picture before he closed the wallet and gave it to her to put on the dresser.

"You wanted to be a reporter, you see," he said, studying her face when she sat down again. "You wanted the city. I wasn't about to put myself in the position of losing out to a career. So I scotched down what I was starting to feel for you, and I found a reason to hate you. That kept you from looking deeper."

She felt her breath stop in her throat. He'd been starting to feel something for her. He hadn't known how she felt, but he was sure she wanted a career instead of marriage. What an irony.

"I...went to Chicago so I wouldn't wear my heart out on you," she confessed. "We all thought you'd marry Barbara someday because she was rich like you, and beautiful and sophisticated."

"Bull," he said curtly. "She was a decorator piece, great for standing in ballrooms and taking to expensive restaurants. I had in mind a woman who'd like being pregnant by me and spending her life looking at cattle and dust and hay."

Her lips parted. "Oh."

"The family ranch, like the family farm, is becoming a thing of the past, Kate, and do you know why? It's because people on farms aren't having a lot of kids anymore. It's unfashionable. They have a son or two, and the son hates the country, so he leaves. Dad grows old and sells the farm." He pursed his lips, letting his dark eyes travel slowly over Kate's tall, slender body. "We could make a lot of babies together."

She gasped. And he laughed, wickedly, seductively, watching her like a hawk.

"Little cowboys," he said softly. "Little cowgirls. I could even learn to change diapers and give bottles, unless you wanted to nurse the babies." His dark eyes went to her breasts and he felt himself going rigid with sweet memories. "Oh, God, Kate, I'd love to watch you nurse them," he whispered fervently.

She was shaking by now. She loved him so desperately. And he wanted children; children would bind them. But even as she wanted it, would have died for it, she realized that their marriage would be only a travesty, with all the love on her side. Someday, inevitably, Jacob would fall in love with someone else and he'd leave her. Nothing would alter that. Her love alone wasn't enough to build a future on.

"No." She forced the word out without looking directly at him. "I'm sorry. I can't." She turned back toward the door.

"You love me, damn it!" he said, exasperated.

"Love on one side isn't enough," she said miserably. "It wouldn't be enough for you, eventually. Someday you'll realize that it was just desire shadowed with pity, Jacob." She opened the door, hiding the tears she couldn't let him see. "Good night."

When she closed the door behind her, he was cursing steadily, watching her go with a kind of impotence he'd never felt. Damn women, damn female logic, damn it all! If he'd felt halfway well, and if she'd been completely healed, he'd have argued away all her protests. But as things stood, he couldn't do anything. He lay back on the pillows with a weary sigh and closed his eyes.

He could have told Kate he loved her, he supposed. The words didn't even feel uncomfortable. But she was certain that his conscience was responsible for how he felt, and that wasn't true. And desire wasn't the only emotion he felt. A man didn't carry a woman's photo around with him for years out of desire alone. But he wasn't quite ready to deal with that much emotion. Not yet. Only, if he didn't do something fast, Kate was going to walk right out of his life. And he couldn't deal with that at all.

He slept on those troubled thoughts, and woke up with a fresh idea. Perhaps he should change tactics.

Kate was at the breakfast table, her face pale, her eyes a little puffy, as if she'd cried all night. He sighed, looking at her eyes. Incredible, that stubborn streak in her. She was still protecting him from himself. Or trying to.

"Want to see your greenhouse today?" Jacob asked, grinning at his father as he took his place at the head of the table and dragged the bacon platter closer. He was still a little hoarse and weak, but he wasn't about to let those minor irritations get him down. He was well on the way to normal.

"Greenhouse?" Kate echoed with her coffee cup halfway to her lips. She brightened immediately. "You mean they're through with it?"

"Haven't you missed the hammering for the past day?" Jacob teased gently. "Yes, they're through. And just in time, because the first snow isn't far away now. I've had them add an emergency generator and a heating system, so that you won't have to worry about power failures. If you get busy, you'll have strawberries in December."

"Strawberries in December." She sighed. But then she looked at him and her face fell as she realized that in December she wouldn't be here anymore. She'd been noble and turned him down. She'd be back in Chicago looking for work, and pretty soon. Her month was almost up.

"What's that sad look for?" he asked.

"I'll be gone," she said. "In December, I mean."

"No, you won't," he said good-humoredly. "We're getting married."

"We are not!" she tossed back, setting her lips into a thin line. "We went over all that last night, Jacob."

"You did, but I didn't." He added eggs to his plate and a biscuit thick with apple butter. "Pour me some coffee, will you, honey?"

"That's the way, son. Just ignore whatever Kate says and marry her anyway," Hank agreed. "Well, Kate," he coaxed when she glared at him, "you have to understand how desperate Janet and I are to marry him off.

He's been in a better humor altogether since you've been on the place. We wouldn't want him to revert to type, would we?''

"I don't care what he reverts to. I can't marry him," Kate said doggedly.

"He's rich," Hank coaxed. "Handsome. He'd spoil you rotten. You'd have lots of kids and I'd get to baby-sit them...."

"Like hell you would," Jacob shot back. "I'm not having you teach my sons how to shoot pool and play blackjack and drink whiskey!"

"Well, it never hurt you none, Jay," Hank said reasonably.

"He let you drink whiskey when you were a little boy?" Kate asked Jacob with wide, curious eyes.

"Of course he did," he muttered. "He let us do anything we wanted. That way we didn't use his whiskey bottles for targets and put burrs in his sheets at night."

"You little monster," Kate accused.

"I had my good points," Jacob replied, finishing his breakfast.

"Did you?" Hank said, puzzled.

"I love you, too," Jacob muttered at him.

"I'm glad, but it's Kate you ought to be practicing on. Why don't you take her to see that greenhouse?" Hank suggested with raised brows and a grin.

"I did have that in mind. I don't need any heavy-handed pushes, thanks."

"Suit yourself, son," Hank said innocently, and bent over his eggs.

Jacob swallowed the rest of his coffee and, noticing that Kate, too, had finished her breakfast, drew her chair out for her and led her down the hall toward the back door.

"Going to show Kate the greenhouse, are you?" Janet asked with a grin, looking from one to the other approvingly. "Nice day for it."

Jacob said something under his breath and herded Kate out the back door.

"Janet is one of a kind." Kate laughed, looking up at him.

"Thank God," he said without a pause.

She shook her head. "It's like an armed camp around here. Do you and Janet and your father fight all the time?"

"Only during daylight." He linked her fingers into his and smiled down at her. It was a sunny, warm day, unseasonably so, and he was in his shirtsleeves. She was wearing jeans, as he was, and a blue print shirt much like the one that covered his broad chest and muscular arms.

"We match," she said without thinking.

"Indeed we do." His hand tightened. "We'll find we have a lot in common. We both love the land, we're dyed-in-the-wool conservationists and, if I remember, you even like animals."

"It isn't enough. Please don't harass me, Jacob," she asked quietly. "It's not fair."

"You want to marry me."

"More than anything," she agreed, her voice husky and soft. "Except your happiness."

"Stubborn woman," he sighed.

"I guess I am. And I haven't even told you how grateful I am that you let me come here to get back on my feet."

"Don't be absurd," he bit off as they reached the huge greenhouse. "I don't want gratitude."

"Jacob, this is awfully big," she said dubiously.

"I told you I had a few experiments of my own in mind." He opened the door for her and she walked inside, aghast at the amount of space she was going to have. The aisles were covered with pine shavings, and there were tables the length of the building. Hoses were connected everywhere, seed starters were sitting in boxes along the walls. Kate just shook her head, awed.

"I never expected anything like this. Oh, Jacob, it's... heavenly!"

He smiled. "I'm glad you like it."

"Like it!" She turned impulsively and hugged him. "You're wonderful!"

He *felt* wonderful with her soft body pressed against him and her face bright and radiant. His hands went to her shoulders to hold her lightly, and his breath caught. It was like flying. His head spun when she touched him.

"You're welcome," he said at her temple.

His faint reticence got through to her and she started to draw away, embarrassed. But when she looked up and saw the indecision in his face, she stood still.

"You've never touched me voluntarily before," he said quietly.

She smiled hesitantly. "I don't suppose I have," she confessed. "You always seemed to have an invisible Keep Away sign around your neck."

"And now I haven't?" he persisted.

"Well... it's less noticeable," she mused.

"Then since it is," he murmured, bending, "why don't you kiss me?"

Her breath caught. That tender note in his deep, drawling voice was new, too. She closed her eyes as his mouth came close enough to capture her own, and then she held on and put her heart into it.

Seconds later, he was the one who drew back, all too quickly.

"We'd better look at some seed catalogs," he said through his teeth, and the eyes that looked down at her were dark with hunger. "Before all my good resolutions go up in smoke."

"Yes." Since she'd refused to marry him, she supposed he didn't feel entitled to make love to her anymore. That was vaguely disappointing, but she had to face reality. This was how it was going to be from now on.

But if she expected him to get better humored as the days went by, she was doomed to disappointment. His temper became shorter and his irritation grew as he drew away from any physical contact at all.

Eleven

Kate spent most of her free time puttering in the greenhouse while Jacob tried to work himself to death. Things were relatively peaceful for three days. And then, on the fourth morning, Jacob sat down at the breakfast table in a black study.

He glared at her as she paused in the doorway in her pale yellow slacks and blouse. "I don't give a damn if you don't want to marry me," he said out of the blue. "Go back to Chicago and get shot at, for all I care."

"Thanks, I will," she returned, sitting in the chair Hank had pulled out for her. "I'm glad to see you're feeling like your old irritable self, Jacob."

"These eggs have curdled, for sure," Janet grumbled as she put them down roughly in front of Jacob. "I've never in my life seen a man in such a bad temper. Kate, I wish you'd marry him and put him out of his misery."

"Me, too," Hank sighed, glancing at her. "Janet and I would never forget you for making the sacrifice."

"I don't want to marry her anymore," Jacob muttered, hacking at his bacon. "This bacon is too hard!"

"Then why don't you go out and cut yourself a piece of beef off one of your cows and eat that?" Janet snapped back.

"And the eggs taste like leather."

"I knew you'd curdle them," the housekeeper returned. She put her hands on her hips and scowled at him. "And I'll bet the coffee's too weak and the biscuits are too crumbly to suit you, too!"

"As a matter of fact, yes," Jacob said.

"Then you can get breakfast in Blairsville in the morning," Janet replied, "because you won't get any here!"

"I'll fire you!" he shot at her.

"Go ahead. I couldn't get a worse boss in hell!"

Jacob put down his fork, glared at everyone and stormed out of the room.

"Thank God, now we can eat in peace," Hank said with a sigh. He smiled at Kate, who was a little paler than normal. "Still holding out, are you?"

"He doesn't love me," she said doggedly. "I won't tie him down. He thinks it's what he wants, but someday he may fall in love."

Hank didn't say a word. But he was smiling as he bent over his eggs.

It was the day that Kate was due to go in for her one-month checkup. She was sure Hank would be deputized to take her, or one of the men, but it was Jacob who waited for her in the Lincoln at the front steps.

He looked out of sorts, as he had for days. He glared, as he had for days. But he opened the door for her, and was as coolly polite as a host could be.

"I guess you'll be headed back to Chicago in no time once you've got the all clear from the doctor," he said as they went lazily down the highway.

"I guess so," she responded without much pleasure. She didn't relish the thought of picking up where she'd left off. The memories were too fresh.

"Don't expect another proposal from me," he continued shortly, "because you aren't getting one."

"I didn't expect to." She stared out at the rolling landscape. The horizon seemed to be years away, and there was such a feeling of spaciousness, of freedom here in South Dakota. She wondered how she'd lived without it. But she shouldn't get too used to it; she was leaving soon. She might as well get used to not seeing Jacob, too, because in no time her precious few weeks with him would be a sweet memory. She felt empty already, and she hadn't even left.

He stopped suddenly in the middle of the deserted highway, and turned to her. "Is it because I've made sex into some kind of nightmare for you?" he asked abruptly, ignoring her flush. "Is that it? Are you afraid to trust your body to me again because I hurt you so badly?"

She felt on fire. "Jacob, I don't want to talk about it, please!"

"Just tell me the truth."

She closed her eyes. "You didn't hurt me that badly," she said through clenched teeth. "It's not because I'm afraid of you."

"So you keep saying." He sighed roughly and eased down on the accelerator. His expression didn't waver as he turned onto the road that led to Blairsville, and he didn't speak again.

The doctor checked her over, pronounced her fit enough to return to work and smiled as she left his office. Jacob paid the bill, against her protests, and led her back to the Lincoln.

"I'm well," she said. "I can go back to work, officially."

"Well, hooray," he muttered as he put her in, got in beside her and started the car.

"You can stop feeling guilty now," she said under her breath, sitting rigidly in her seat. "I don't hold anything that happened against you, all right?"

He wasn't listening. The day was unseasonably warm, and he turned off onto a dirt road that led deep into the woods, to a secluded little glade where a stream bubbled across the road and the wind blew through a small stand of trees.

"Why are we stopping here?" she asked uneasily.

He turned to her, his dark eyes blazing. "Because I'm sick to death of having you try to save me from myself. Why in hell do you think I want to marry you out of guilt and pity? I'm not stupid enough to try and build a long-term relationship on that kind of emotional quicksand!"

She tried to speak, and stammered, "Then, why?"

"I like being with you," he said curtly. "God knows why, you drive me nuts most of the time. I like doing things with you, I even like being alone with you." He searched her face slowly. "I'd even like to have kids with you. Despite the bad beginning we had, we've grown pretty close since you've been at Warlance, Kate. Close enough to gamble on marriage. At least, I think so."

She could hardly think at all. He was knocking down her arguments one by one. "I want to marry you," she whispered brokenly. "I want it more than anything on earth, Jacob. But it's such a risk, don't you see?"

"All I see," he whispered back, "is a body I ache for in the darkness, a mind that matches mine thought for thought and a woman I'd kill for."

Holding her eyes with his, he slid the seat back and unfastened first his seat belt, then hers. He moved closer without saying a word, but the expression in his dark eyes was speaking as he bent to her mouth.

It was the slowest, softest kiss they'd ever shared. She felt his arms enclosing her, his fingers easing into her hair to hold her head where he wanted it as he began to deepen the kiss.

She made one token protest that turned into a soft moan, and then she yielded to his tenderness. Birds called back and forth, the bubbling stream made itself heard even through the closed windows. The wind blew softly. But Kate was feeling his hands touching her, turning her, gently discovering her. She was hearing Jacob's rough breath against her soft mouth, and feeling his heartbeat against her breasts.

He turned her, moving her so that she was lying on the seat. Vaguely she heard him opening a door to make more room. The bubbling sound increased, like her heartbeat. She looked up at him—breathless, curious, searching.

She started to speak, but he smiled and shook his head. He bent again to her warm lips and began to nibble at them.

His hands eased her blouse out of his way, so that he had access to her lacy bra. That, too, was easily disposed of. His mouth was on that soft skin, nibbling, tasting, covering first one taut breast and then the other in a silence that grew hot with expectation.

It was a lesson in arousal. She'd never realized how many nerves she had in her body, or how sensitive they were to a man's hands and mouth. He smoothed his lips over her skin like hands, and she didn't feel her slacks and briefs slide down her legs, because his mouth was like a narcotic. She couldn't get enough of it.

His shirt was gone and she was touching him in all the ways she'd wanted to. He guided her hands down his sides, and she discovered somewhere along the way that his jeans were loose and pushed away as well.

His forearms were taking most of his weight when he moved against her and her eyes opened, misty and soft and inquiring.

"It's broad daylight," she whispered, gasping as she realized where they were, with both doors open in the middle of a field.

"So it is," he mused softly, moving even closer. "Broad daylight, and no secrets between us. And I want you to the point of madness. I want you to see how much, feel how much." He bent to her mouth, cherishing it with aching tenderness, and his heart beat roughly over her taut breasts.

"Jacob, we mustn't..." she whispered, but she moaned as well, because her body was throbbing with arousal.

"I want you for my wife, Kathryn," he breathed against her ardent mouth. "I want you to be the mother of my children. I'm not asking you to give yourself a second time without a commitment. I'm asking you for the rest of your life. And I'm going to show you what beauty there can be in intimacy when two people share it unselfishly."

She could feel how hungry he was. His body was keeping no secrets from her. She searched his dark eyes. "It isn't . . . just desire?"

He smiled gently. "If that was all it was, any woman would do," he said quietly.

"And any woman won't?" she persisted breathlessly.

His mouth brushed her eyes, her nose. "I don't want anybody except you, Kate. There isn't going to be another woman, ever."

"Oh, Jacob, you might fall in love. . . ." she moaned.

"Yes," he said against her parted lips, "I might at that. Lie still, sweet, and let me love you. Let me show you how it should have been that first time."

She didn't answer him. She didn't have to. Her long, slender legs moved, just enough to admit the vibrant masculinity of his body.

"This time," he whispered into her mouth as he began to bite at it sensuously, "you and I are going to fly into the sun together."

"Someone might come here. . . ." she protested with her last logical thought.

"No." He moved, ever so gently, and his eyes held hers as she felt the first tender probing of his body. He saw her gasp, felt her hands grasp his arms. "Relax for me," he whispered. "I promise, it isn't going to hurt at all. Join with me, Kate. Let your body be one with mine."

She bit her lower lip. She was thinking of all the reasons why she shouldn't.

He knew that. His hand moved down, and she gasped at the sudden throbbing wave of passion that trembled over her skin. "Don't think," he whispered. "Just lie back and let me do it all. Let me give you pleasure. Let me teach you."

She was trembling. He moved, careful not to jar her too much, and she felt him as she had that night. Only now it wasn't hurting. Her eyes grew wide with every slow, adept movement of his hips, and he watched her the whole time, adjusting his motions to the needs of her soft body under him. He whispered things—sweet, shocking things—and his hands guided her with unbearable patience, until she was as wild for him as he was for her.

She bit back a sharp moan and he smiled through his own hunger, because he knew what that meant—that sound, and the sudden twisting of her body and the dilation of her eyes. Yes, she was feeling it now. He moved more deeply, more fiercely, and she closed her eyes and began to make noises that incited him.

His hair-matted chest rubbed with sweet abrasion against her bare breasts as he increased the rhythm, and the sounds outside were drowned by the sounds inside.

She was whispering things to him now, secret things, and he laughed and bit her shoulder, her mouth, her throat as the spiraling tension caught them both up in a whirlwind of warm pleasure.

Her eyes opened as the coil began to tighten suddenly. His face was damp with sweat and his jaw was clenched and he was breathing fiercely above her. She matched his movements, reached up to him and, as her fingers touched his face, it all exploded.

Magic. Madness. The sun, blazing colors, roaring surf, a feverish crashing together that brought with it the first rapture of her life. The first anguished burst of ecstasy. The first fulfillment.

She came back very slowly to the sounds of the trees and the wind and the birds. She was shaking, and so was he. His heartbeat was heavy over her breasts, his body had a fine tremor.

She began to kiss his throat, his chin, his hard mouth, and he returned the caress with satisfying ferocity.

"Sweet," he whispered roughly, his eyes blazing into hers. "Pleasure beyond bearing. I thought I might die trying to hold you to me."

"Yes." She touched his mouth with wonder, searched his eyes. Her breath caught. "Jacob...you didn't..." She swallowed. "There could be a child."

He smiled lazily. "Yes." He kissed her closed eyelids, her nose, her mouth. "I'm sleepy."

"So am I." She brushed back his thick, dark hair. "What are we going to do?"

"Get married, of course," he murmured. "And I'm not asking you, Kate. You'll damned well have to do it without a proposal, because I'm not giving you a chance to turn me down again."

He was offering heaven, especially after what they'd just shared. Her worried eyes searched his. "You might fall in love someday," she whispered for the second time.

He kissed her eyes shut. "What did we just share, if it wasn't love?" he whispered.

Her eyelids came open again, and she was staring at him.

He hadn't meant to say that. It had just popped out. But as he looked down at her lovely face, he could believe that he'd meant it. Sex had never been like this before. He brushed back her hair. "No heavy thoughts right now," he whispered. "Kiss me."

She did, warmly, softly, and then he moved reluctantly away and helped her dress with exquisite tenderness. In between soft kisses, he gathered up his own disheveled clothing and got it in order again.

He sat back, smoking a cigarette, while she stared at him from the shelter of his arm.

"I didn't hurt your rib?" he asked belatedly, search-ing her face.

She shook her head. "I wouldn't have noticed even if you did."

He hugged her close. "Thank God. And have we re-moved a few scars in the process?" he asked gently, searching her eyes. "Have I made up for that night?"

She flushed. "Yes."

"From now on, it gets better every time. Next week we're getting married, and have I got a wedding present for you, young Kate," he added with a secretive smile.

"What is it?" she asked.

"Wait and see," he mused, and kissed her again, tast-ing nectar on her mouth. He sighed. "Now, no more second thoughts. Nobody's forcing me to the altar. All right?"

She searched his face, loving him too much to refuse again. All her noble principles had gone up in smoke in his arms. He was addictive. She couldn't give him up.

"All right, Jacob," she breathed.

He smiled after a minute, and pulled her closer.

The wedding ceremony was performed at Warlance, and Margo and David attended, surprised and delighted to find two old enemies exchanging rings.

Jacob beamed at his lovely bride in her acres of white satin and lace, and amid baskets of flowers they ex-changed their vows, with Hank and Janet and Margo and David and Tom and a scattering of neighbors in atten-dance, including a strange city-looking woman in a blue hat sitting all alone.

The rings in place, the vows spoken solemnly, Jacob removed her veil and kissed her gently. The ceremony had been so beautiful that she cried. If he'd loved her, it would have been heaven itself. But, she told herself, she couldn't ask for the moon.

"Imagine, you and Uncle Jacob getting married," Margo whispered during a brief pause in Kate's bedroom. "I thought you hated each other."

"So did we," Kate grinned, changing into a pink dress for the small reception. There wasn't time for a honeymoon, but it didn't matter. Jacob had promised her Paris in the spring.

"Did you notice that elderly woman in the audience—the one with the blue hat? I thought she was Ben Hamlin's sister, but nobody seems to know her."

Kate pursed her lips. She'd noticed the woman, all right. There had been something vaguely familiar about her. Perhaps she was an old neighbor who'd moved away, or some acquaintance of the family.

"Speak of the devil," Margo murmured wickedly when they opened the door and saw the heavyset woman in the blue hat coming toward the bedroom. She had on just a touch of makeup, and she was rather attractive even for her age. She was nervous, too, twisting a handkerchief out of shape in her slender hands.

"Kathryn?"

Kate blinked. So the woman did know her. "Yes?"

"Excuse me, I'll go find David," Margo said and left the room.

The woman in the hat searched eyes as green as her own. "You don't know me, do you?" she asked hesitantly and her eyes brimmed with tears. "How could I expect you to? He stole you away from me when you were just a baby...."

Kate's eyes widened. She stared at the older version of herself. No wonder the woman had seemed so familiar.

All the long years of hatred and bitterness and anguish came back and boiled over.

"You deserted us," Kate accused furiously. "You left us, and he beat me, he beat Tom!"

The older woman stared at her helplessly with tears stinging down her cheeks. She tried to speak, failed, tried again. "He stole you, Kathryn. Took you away and hid you, and I had nothing. No money, no place to live... I'd sneaked away to get a lawyer, so I could divorce him and get custody of you and Tom. There was a man, a sweet, gentle man, who wanted you both and would have been so good to us after that... that creature your father became—" She sobbed and caught her breath. "I had it all worked out, and then he found out, and before I could get back out to the farm, he was gone." She pressed the handkerchief against her eyes. "He was gone with both my babies, and I didn't even have the price of a bus ticket to try and find you."

Kate heard the words with a sense of unreality. She stared at her mother blankly. This wasn't how her poor, tormented father had related the past.

"He... stole us?"

"Stole you, my sweet," the older woman said huskily. She stared at her daughter with eyes full of pride and love and pain. "I waited tables in a bar for two years to save enough money to start looking, but by then it was too late."

"And the man, the one you were going to marry?" Kate prodded.

"I turned him away," came the unexpected reply. "I had a horrible feeling about what you and Tom were going through, Kathryn. How could I be so callous as to build my happiness on your pain?"

Kate took a slow breath, vaguely aware of Jacob watching from the other room. She searched her mother's eyes. "You've been alone all this time?"

"All this time," her mother replied softly. "I'd already exhausted all the government agencies, and I'd long ago forgotten that your father's mother lived in South Dakota. He'd hardly ever mentioned her. And then, your new husband came into the restaurant where I work and told me that you and Tom were alive and that he'd bring me to see you." The tears started again through a smile. "I haven't stopped crying for days. I don't care if you hate me; it's enough just to be able to look at you."

"Oh, Mama, don't—"

Kate went into the older woman's arms as if there hadn't been a single day between the past and the present. She rocked her, comforted her, and felt the pain slowly dissolving as she realized what it must have been like all the long years. At least she'd had Tom. Their mother had had no one, only a terrible fear for her children and loneliness.

Tom was beside Jacob now, grinning, and when Kate saw him, she realized that the two of them must have been plotting this together. When Tom joined them, their mother drew him close, too.

"My boy," she wept. "My baby boy. When I first saw you, I could hardly believe so much time had passed. And now I've found you, and Kate, and it's like a dream. Like another dream, and I'm so afraid I'll wake up, as I usually do, and find you gone."

"We won't be gone, Mama." Tom laughed. "Neither will you. Kate and I will shuttle you back and forth between South Dakota and New York for a while before we let you go home."

"Of course we will," Kate agreed, pulling back to borrow her mother's handkerchief and dry her red eyes.

"I'd love that," their mother said, beaming. "I really would. And then I think I may say yes to the man who's been proposing for the past twenty-two years—"

Kate gasped. "He's still waiting for you, after all these years?"

"Love doesn't wear out, Katie," her mother said with a wise, world-weary smile. "Not if it's real. Yes. He's still waiting. And so was I, until I found my babies."

"Some babies." Tom grinned at his sister.

"Speaking of which," Jacob mused, joining them to slide a possessive arm around Kate's shoulders, "I hope you like grandchildren. Kate and I have a large family in mind."

"I'd love that." Mrs. Walker sighed, glancing from one to the other. "And right now, I'd like to wash my face. I must look a mess."

"You look just like your children to me," Jacob replied, "but help yourself."

"Yes, and then hurry back. We've got so much to talk about," Kate said gently.

"I'll do that." Mrs. Walker touched Kate's hair, and Tom's cheek, and went off into the bedroom, sniffling a little.

"Oh, Jacob," Kate sighed, studying her new husband. "How long did you plan this?"

"A couple of weeks. Tom helped." He smiled. "We thought you might want to see what having a mother was like."

"I'm so glad," she said warmly, and hugged Tom. "Isn't she nice?"

"Our mother would have to be," Tom chided. "Now, excuse me while I grab some punch. My throat's apt to get dry from talking so much when we start this new family reunion.''

"Are you happy?" Jacob asked quietly, studying Kate. "It was a hell of a gamble, but it seems to have come off without a hitch.''

"For all those years, I blamed her when she was as miserable as we were.'' She sighed, staring up at him. "How could I have been so blind?''

"Aren't we all blind, from time to time?'' he asked. He touched her hair softly, loving its silky feel. She was beautiful in her neat dress, and he looked as if he could die just looking at her. She was his now, and all the barriers seemed to come down at once. He drew her to one side of the hall, away from prying eyes, and held her there.

"I was blind about you, wasn't I, Kate? I never had any idea how much you cared about me until I saw all those photos you kept of me....'' He took a steadying breath and his jaw tautened. "My God,'' he breathed, his hands hurting her a little where they held her upper arms, "you'll never know what I went through those first twenty-four hours after you were shot. My world went black. If anything had happened to you, I don't know how in hell I'd have stayed alive.''

She wasn't sure that she was hearing him. Her eyes stared blankly at his hard face, hanging on every word.

"You felt responsible,'' she whispered. "There was no need to feel that way.''

"I...loved you,'' he whispered, biting off the words with a kind of pain he couldn't hold back any longer. His gaze fell to her bodice, so that she wouldn't see his eyes. "For a long time. But I'd seen what love did to men, giving women a hold. My own mother tormented Hank half to death because he loved her. I wasn't going to let that happen to me. So I convinced myself it was only desire, and once I had you, it would fade away."

He laughed bitterly, lifting tormented eyes to hers. "But it didn't get better, Kate. I went home and got drunk and stayed drunk, and still I could hear you crying." He shifted restlessly, his eyes hungry on her rapt face. "And then I was going to go back and have it out, but you got shot. Then Tom told me everything." His eyes closed. "And the light went out of the world."

She touched his face tentatively, hesitantly, her fingers trembling. "Oh, Jacob!"

His eyes opened, blazing with possession. "I love you," he whispered roughly. "I always have. So you see, Kate, there's not really much danger of my falling in love with anyone else."

She didn't try to answer. She reached up and put her mouth softly against his hard one. He lifted her against him and held her. He kissed her and she responded with all the lonely hunger of all the long years. His arms were bruising, and she welcomed their involuntary fierceness, because she understood the passion they were betraying. She felt it, too, burned with it, ached with it, and her mouth demanded as much as his own. She moaned suddenly, her legs beginning to tremble, and he pulled back.

His hard face was taut with passion. "I want you," he whispered roughly. "I want you the way it was that day in the front seat of my car, so tender and slow that I thought I'd die of the pleasure. I want to make love with you and know that you love me as much as I love you."

She touched her mouth to his chin, his neck, trembling with shared emotion. "I want that, too," she breathed. "I never dreamed it would happen, that you'd be able to care for me, ever."

His hands smoothed her dark hair, ruffling it. "Not even when I showed you your picture in my wallet?" he murmured against her throat.

"That was the only hope I had," she whispered. "That, and the way you practically threw Roger Dean out of my room in the hospital."

He lifted his hand, his eyes fierce. "I wanted to throw him out the window," he returned. "You were mine. I didn't want any other man near you."

"There never will be." She sighed. She leaned back against his encircling arms. "I like children," she said.

He smiled. "So do I."

She smiled slowly. "Well?"

"Don't tempt me," he muttered, bending to kiss her hungrily. "Wedding guests never go home," he groaned.

"You're the one who insisted on inviting so many," she whispered against his lips.

"Damn my own stupidity," he murmured.

"We can have punch and cake—"

"I don't want punch and cake. I want acres of bed and you in the middle of it, even if all we do is hold each other...."

"Now cut that out, you two," Tom called. His mother was holding his arm as he confronted Jacob and Kate with a mischievous grin. "You've got your whole lives to do that, but only a few precious hours to spend with your family before I spirit Mom off to New York with me."

"I guess you're right," Jacob said, damping down the fires. He smiled warmly at Kate. "We have the rest of our lives together."

Kate pushed back her disheveled hair, never more beautiful, with her green eyes sparkling and her face bright with love and laughter. "What a beautiful thought," she whispered to Jacob.

He took her hand and brought it to his lips. "Isn't it, though?" he said with a grin. And as he led her along the hall behind Tom and Mrs. Walker, Kate felt as if she were walking on dreams the whole way.

*   *   *   *   *

Don't miss the reissue of Diana Palmer's HEATHER'S SONG, coming in March from the exciting new Silhouette Classics line! Starting in November, we're bringing back your old favorites written by authors who have come to be your special friends. Don't miss it!

Take 4 Silhouette Special Edition novels and a surprise gift

FREE

Then preview 6 brand-new books—delivered to your door as soon as they come off the presses! If you decide to keep them, you pay just $2.49 each*—a 9% saving off the retail price, *with no additional charges for postage and handling!*

Romance is alive, well and flourishing in the moving love stories of Silhouette Special Edition novels. They'll awaken your desires, enliven your senses and leave you tingling all over with excitement.

Start with 4 Silhouette Special Edition novels and a surprise gift absolutely FREE. They're yours to keep without obligation. You can always return a shipment and cancel at any time.

Simply fill out and return the coupon today!

* Plus 69¢ postage and handling per shipment in Canada.

Silhouette Special Edition®

Silhouette Romance™

Legendary Lovers Trilogy

BY DEBBIE MACOMBER....

ONCE UPON A TIME, in a land not so far away, there lived a girl, Debbie Macomber, who grew up dreaming of castles, white knights and princes on fiery steeds. Her family was an ordinary one with a mother and father and one wicked brother, who sold copies of her diary to all the boys in her junior high class.

One day, when Debbie was only nineteen, a handsome electrician drove by in a shiny black convertible. Now Debbie knew a prince when she saw one, and before long they lived in a two-bedroom cottage surrounded by a white picket fence.

As often happens when a damsel fair meets her prince charming, children followed, and soon the two-bedroom cottage became a four-bedroom castle. The kingdom flourished and prospered, and between soccer games and car pools, ballet classes and clarinet lessons, Debbie thought about love and enchantment and the magic of romance.

One day Debbie said, "What this country needs is a good fairy tale." She remembered how well her diary had sold and she dreamed again of castles, white knights and princes on fiery steeds. And so the stories of Cinderella, Beauty and the Beast, and Snow White were reborn....

Look for Debbie Macomber's *Legendary Lovers* trilogy from Silhouette Romance: *Cindy and the Prince* (January, 1988); *Some Kind of Wonderful* (March, 1988); *Almost Paradise* (May, 1988). Don't miss them!

SRT-1

ATTRACTIVE, SPACE SAVING BOOK RACK

Display your most prized novels on this handsome and sturdy book rack. The hand-rubbed walnut finish will blend into your library decor with quiet elegance, providing a practical organizer for your favorite hard-or soft-covered books.

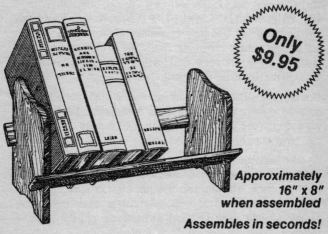

Only $9.95

Approximately 16" x 8" when assembled

Assembles in seconds!

To order, rush your name, address and zip code, along with a check or money order for $10.70* ($9.95 plus 75¢ postage and handling) payable to *Silhouette Books*.

Silhouette Books
Book Rack Offer
901 Fuhrmann Blvd.
P.O. Box 1396
Buffalo, NY 14269-1396

Offer not available in Canada.

*New York and Iowa residents add appropriate sales tax.

BKR-2A

 # Silhouette Desire

COMING NEXT MONTH

#397 TO LOVE AGAIN—Lass Small
After a personal tragedy, Felicia's feelings were totally numb—and she intended to keep them that way. But Nate wasn't about to let a will of steel come between him and the woman he loved.

#398 WEATHERING THE STORM—Elaine Camp
Simon wanted no part of the past he'd shared with Marlee. But she had a foolproof plan to change his mind. Simon was no fool, and he found that together they could weather any storm.

#399 TO THE HIGHEST BIDDER—Cathryn Clare
Thrown together over possession of a New England farmhouse, Janni and Bart planned to battle it out. Though the house was collateral, they found they couldn't put a price on love.

#400 LIGHTNING STRIKES TWICE—Jane Gentry
Dr. Jake Rowan was back, but Attorney Nola O'Brien wasn't interested. He'd left her heartbroken, but now he was determined to right past wrongs—the answer was love!

#401 BUILT TO LAST—Laurel Evans
Pressures from her job had Allison Napoli looking for an alternative life-style, and architect Josh Fitzpatrick was just the answer. But could he convince her that home was where the heart is?

#402 INDISCREET—Tess Marlowe
When Terri Genetti was forced to close her business, she didn't know handsome entrepreneur Jim Holbrook was behind her problems. But Terri learned she could follow her heart without betraying her dreams.

AVAILABLE NOW:

#391 BETRAYED BY LOVE
Diana Palmer

#392 RUFFLED FEATHERS
Katherine Granger

#393 A LUCKY STREAK
Raye Morgan

#394 A TASTE OF FREEDOM
Candice Adams

#395 PLAYING WITH MATCHES
Ariel Berk

#396 TWICE IN A LIFETIME
BJ James

In response
to last year's outstanding success,
Silhouette Brings You:

Silhouette Christmas Stories 1987

Specially chosen for you in a delightful volume celebrating the holiday season, four original romantic stories written by four of your favorite Silhouette authors.

Dixie Browning—*Henry the Ninth*
Ginna Gray—*Season of Miracles*
Linda Howard—*Bluebird Winter*
Diana Palmer—*The Humbug Man*

Each of these bestselling authors will enchant you with their unforgettable stories, exuding the magic of Christmas and the wonder of falling in love.

A heartwarming Christmas gift during the holiday season...indulge yourself and give this book to a special friend!

Available now

XM87-1R